If the earth should move...

If the earth should move...

and other stories

Deepa Agarwal

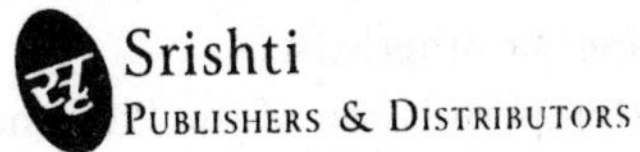
Srishti
Publishers & Distributors

Srishti Publishers & Distributors
64-A, Adhchini
Sri Aurobindo Marg
New Delhi 110 017
srishtipublishers@forindia.com

First published in 2002 by
Srishti Publishers & Distributors

ISBN 81-87075-88-0
Rs. 145.00

Cover Design by Arrt Creations
45 Nehru Apartment, Kalkaji, New Delhi 110 019
arrt@vsnl.com

Printed and bound in India by
Saurabh Print-O-Pack, Noida

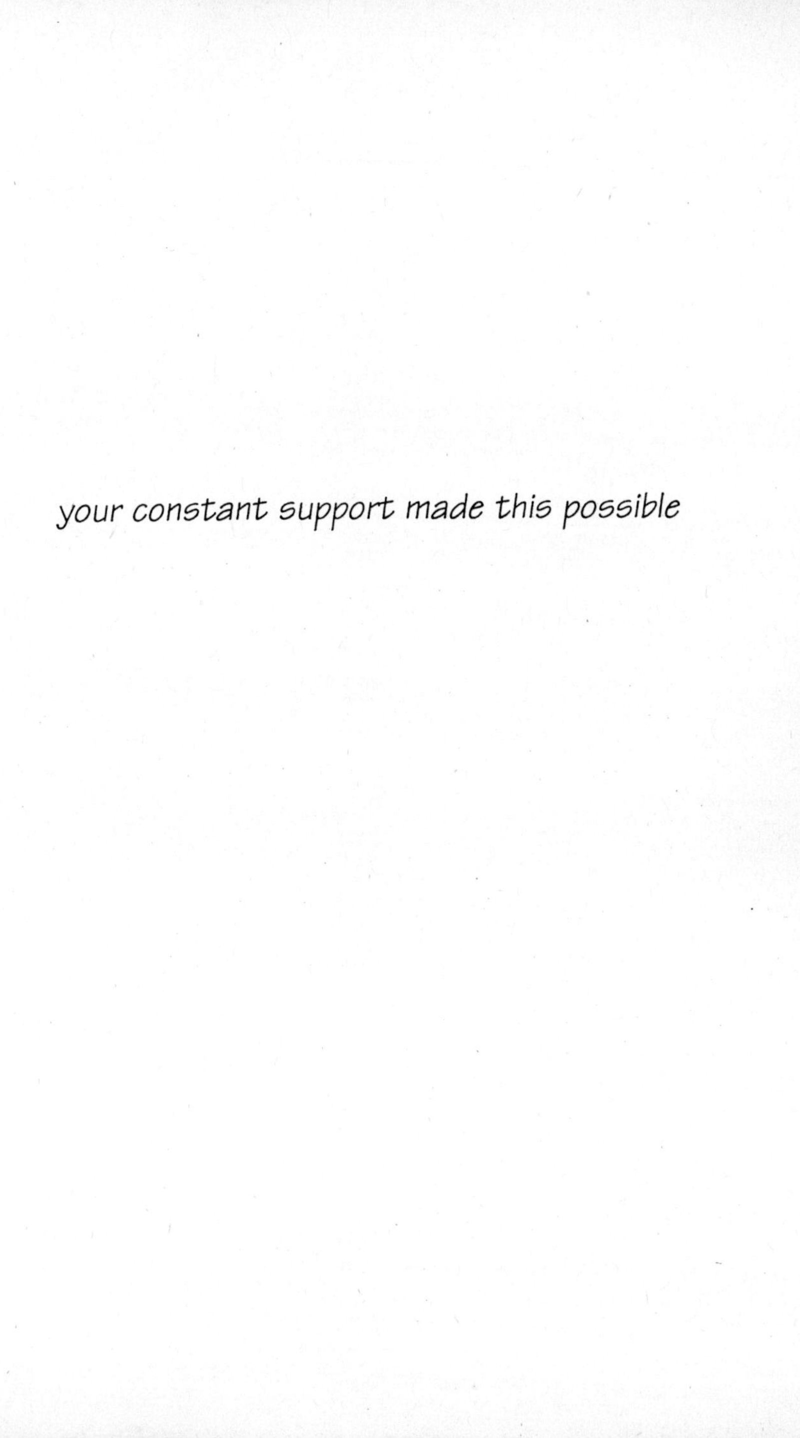
your constant support made this possible

'One tries to go deep-speak to the secret self we all have.'

Katherine Mansfield

ACKNOWLEDGEMENTS

Cradle Song' won the first prize in *The Asian Age* short story competition 1995, 'The Crossing' first appeared in *Manushi*, 'House of Cards' in *Cosmopolitan* and 'You Cannot have all the Answers' in *The Pioneer*.

CONTENTS

CRADLE SONG

Some stories begin at the beginning and some at the end. And in some it's hard to say where the beginning is and where the end ...

This is a story of seven sisters. Seven is a lucky number, no doubt. But I have never heard of seven sisters being considered lucky. Only, if by chance, those seven sisters happen to be blessed with a brother. Then they can, and they are bound to consider themselves lucky beyond all doubt.

My mother was one of those seven sisters. The fourth, the bang-in-the-middle sister, with three older than her and three younger. She was born when my grandmother was beginning to tire a little of only giving birth to daughters. Tire, but not despair. For being a truly determined woman, I don't think she despaired even when the seventh daughter, my Meena *masi* was born.

It was like a battle with destiny for her, I think. A battle she was determined to win at all costs. So grim, stony with purpose, fortified with the accumulated magic of all the prayers, the rituals and fasts which had become a part of her life through all those contentious years; the predictions of numerous astrologers and the blessings of countless saints – even those which had not worked so far – she had tried again. And the son was born, who changed the fate of the seven sisters overnight. From being considered pitiful, almost doomed, they suddenly found themselves blessed.

Such is the power of a male child.

Now in this story of seven lucky sisters, another seven intrudes. The seventh year of the fourth decade of the twentieth century – nineteen forty-seven to be exact. A year written in letters of gold and blood for our country. The most auspicious year of the century for the millions who were freed from foreign rule, and yet a most inauspicious one; for many would call it so. The uprooted ones, those who fled bag and baggage, fire and blood marking their trail, when one country was suddenly split into two.

My mother was eleven when her brother was born – whose birth she had awaited ever since she became aware of the importance of having brothers. She has a vivid memory of the event. The dancing, the singing, the distribution of largesse, the new clothes. She remembers her mother, bedecked, bejeweled, her tired face aglow, rocking the baby in a magnificent new cradle, the best that money could buy.

But just a few months later, the best that money could buy

them was escape and flight, as they hurried, frantic to get away from the house that was no longer shelter but a death trap. To flee the city which was no longer home but hostile territory. Almost everything had to be abandoned, including the cradle, in which the youngest of the sisters had furtively rocked herself when the baby was elsewhere. She had not possessed a new cradle, not even too many new clothes, she mostly wore hand-me-downs. Good quality, expensive hand-me-downs since my grandfather was a prosperous trader. But then, new clothes, new cradles have a smell and a magic of their own, which she had rarely experienced. She was the one who had howled, thrown a tantrum because the cradle had to be left behind. The baby brother of course, did not even know what he was being deprived of.

His mother's lap was soft enough. Her breast was readily offered to soothe him whenever he happened to howl. The motion of the train rocked him all the way. My mother remembers the press, the stench of bodies. The weeping, sometimes low, a bare whimper; sometimes loud, a lament or a wholehearted protest against the fickleness of fortune. She remembers blood-stained clothes, staring eyes and an unreal, distant howling the wind sucked up from God knows where to graze their spines, set them all a-shiver. She remembers the old man who mumbled, thumbing his prayer beads ceaselessly. She thought of his importunities dripping, dripping into the ears of an obdurate deity, like drops of water wearing away a stone. She remembers humming a song to herself to block out all those horrible sounds. The cradlesong that her mother crooned to put her baby brother to sleep. It was the only one she could recall at the moment.

Still, they considered themselves lucky when they arrived, a whole family – the parents, the seven lucky sisters and the luck-producing brother, intact, at the place of refuge. They arrived, their bodies still swaying, rocked by the motion of the train, the sobbing of the bereaved, the cries still ringing in their ears. The memory of the blood-stained garments remained fresh. The journey haunted their dreams, or rather their nightmares, for years.

My grandmother offered repeated prayers of gratitude to the almighty who had let her baby survive that horrendous flight. My mother thought of those prayers as a kind of magic spell, charmed words that protected them against future disaster. She repeated them after her mother, felt safe and cared for.

The baby grew, though my grandmother found the milk in her breasts much reduced. Because of the trauma, perhaps, or the hardships of their new estate. But the baby grew, despite all this, thrived in fact, cared for by seven doting sisters, even the youngest who still missed the cradle and lived in a state of confusion, wondering when they would return to their own home. She talked to the baby, poured out all her puzzlement to him. He replied, babbling in a tongue only she could understand. His answers must have satisfied her, because after a while she reconciled herself to living in a verandah, where cooking, eating, sleeping – everything was done in the same place, instead of in a proper house with separate rooms.

The baby grew and the family, still rocking on their feet, tried to steady themselves, jam those shaky feet into the ground. Plant them firmly, permanently, like a seed that remains fixed in one particular place – so that they could kill the memory of that hateful movement. Like a seed that germinates, bonds itself with the earth, clutching at it with its stubborn insistent roots. Thrusts its growing stem upwards, greedily sucking nurture and sunshine through its spreading leaves.

My grandfather, forgetting what he had possessed in the old country or what he had been, took up whatever work he could. There was that family to feed and ultimately, those seven sisters to think of and provide for. In other words, marry off with decent dowries. Yes, a man with seven daughters can barely pause to take breath, leave alone waste time in bewailing his misfortune. To be fair, the sisters did their bit – at least those of them who were old enough. They knitted, they sewed, they embroidered – dutifully set themselves to any kind of labour that could be turned into money. My mother thought of that work as a mound of coins piling up, growing till it carried them out of the verandah to a proper house and their father from the pavement into a proper shop …

"The marvel is that it actually happened," Mamma says. Her eyes are very shiny. I try to think of her, of my aunts, my grandfather and grandmother, leading difficult, deprived lives. Sometimes it's hard to believe it, looking at the diamonds flashing on their fingers, in their ears. For they are all more or less prosperous, their lives run smoothly on wheels well-oiled with money. But when I watch my mother haggling with a vegetable vendor, reducing him to the rock bottom price with a determination that seems disproportionate, I can feel the motion that swayed her feet, like a faint, disturbing breeze.

All the same, that time was far, far behind in the past; especially for us children, the offspring of the seven lucky sisters. (Oddly enough, all of them had more sons than daughters. It was as if providence was trying to make up for past injustice.) To repeat, the time they had experienced belonged to the stuff of myth and legend for us. Folklore of sorts, a kind of warning of what could happen, but unreal, invariably unreal ... except when somebody wept. Which did happen now and then when the old times were recalled. Which made us feel uncomfortable, even a little annoyed with the person who gave way. Because what was the point of dredging up bad memories, deliberately making oneself unhappy?

So it seemed strange, unbelievable, when one day, Meena *masi*, my youngest aunt, the one who had missed the cradle the most, asked, "Would you like to go home?"

"Go home?" My mother paused in the act of conveying a *samosa* to her mouth. Meena *masi* was visiting, they'd spent a lazy afternoon, just chatting, as they often did, being well-heeled ladies of leisure. "B-but, I'm home, I mean – what do you mean?" She put the *samosa* down; confused, a little perturbed, it seemed to me.

I wondered why, because after all, Meena *masi*, the youngest, prettiest and most prosperous, was a little – well – peculiar. Her doting husband indulged her, her sisters protected her, took care of her. She had been considered the luckiest of the sisters; she'd opened the way for the brother, so desperately longed for – as the old women said. True, this luck had deserted her at one point. But the habit persisted.

"Home ... I said ... Have you forgotten what home was like?" Meena *masi's* eyes were teasingly mysterious as she bit into a *samosa* and licked the chutney from her fingers.

"Home ..." Mamma repeated. Her brow had clouded; she gazed apprehensively at Meena *masi.* "You can't mean ..."

"Yes, I do – the place where we were all born. Would you like to go there, visit it?"

"You can't be serious!"

"I am. Absolutely serious." And anyone could make out from her face that she had never been more serious in her life. "He says, he can make arrangements. He has a contact ..."

'He' of course, was the doting husband, the man who had the ability to make almost any kind of 'arrangement', who possessed almost any kind of useful 'contact'.

I could feel the goose pimples flare up, a prickly rash, like as if I had suddenly brushed against a cactus plant. Mamma looked scared, her face had turned patchy – but how could she say 'No'?

It was the cradle that was drawing her there, I should have guessed. I should have remembered the strange look that came into her eyes when she talked about it, as if it were not an ordinary cradle but a talisman, something magical. Because what memories could that place hold for her, that place that she referred to as 'home'? For, home was here, wasn't it? I find it significant that the other aunts refused. Or rather found some ready excuses not to go. They began to make them even before they were asked. So it made them look quite sheepish when Meena *masi* said, "I wasn't planning to take you all. Even *he* won't be able to make arrangements for so many people."

I managed to tag along. I don't know why I went. I'm not sure if one really wants to know what one's mother's life was before she became your mother. It interferes too much with the image that's familiar, that means mother. But perhaps a time of life comes when the need to know overcomes that insecurity. When one is afraid that the chance will be lost forever if one postpones too much.

Because it did interfere with the image. My mother's hysterical, excited reunion with what remained of the old world that she had known – neighbours, shopkeepers, even an old childhood friend.

Tears were shed. Long buried memories disinterred. Meena *masi* was quiet, though. After having thought about, planned, arranged and anticipated everything – was there a sense of anti-climax? Or not being able to conjure up common memories and renew bonds. Was she feeling a little left out?

It didn't help when I tactlessly whispered, "You couldn't be remembering anything, could you?"

Her eyes flashed with affront. "Of course I do, it's all there … deep inside …"

It was at that very moment that the old lady entered. An amazingly fat old lady, her silks rustling and swishing, panting and sweating from excitement and exertion. "Kanta! Kanta, is it really you? Ah, what a miracle! I heard that you were here. I couldn't believe it! No one, no one has come back – even for a visit."

"Saida *bua*! It's Saida *bua*!" Mamma exclaimed. "It's hard," she sighed. "Almost impossible …" The rest of her words were squashed out by Saida *bua's* embrace.

"Who's this? Not Meena, not little Meena … And – your daughter? Amazing, wonderful!" More embraces, laughter and tears. Then she paused, pinned Mamma with a look full of happy, satisfied meaning. "Come, come on, you have to come to my house. At once!" she commanded, taking my mother's hand, almost dragging her away. Helpless, laughing, Mamma allowed herself to be led. We followed, bemused.

"I have something to show you," she muttered. "You'll get such a surprise. Your mother should have come. Why didn't you bring her?"

Mamma mumbled the same excuse she had been giving to everyone. Old age, the rigours of travel, the danger of too much excitement … Meena *masi* frowned, touched her forehead delicately. As if all this talk was giving her a headache. We sat down gingerly on the plush sofa, swallowed more syrupy sherbet, nibbled at some more sweets.

"You won't believe it …" Saida *bua* sighed. "You know…after you all went away …" she broke off abruptly, as if reconsidering the suitability of what she was about to say. Then ended by muttering, "Ah, what a dreadful time it was … terrible, unbelievable.The looting, the destruction…But I managed – " She threw a quick glance at Mamma's face, which was turning grim and hurriedly switched tracks to say, "Your daughter looks just like your mother. What a lovely woman – so brave so generous … *Oye*, Rehman, bring it fast!" she yelled suddenly.

Meena *masi* blinked, sat up nervously, when we heard the sound of something being dragged down the stairs. Something heavy, something wooden?

"Let it be, let it be," Mamma half rose, with smiling politeness. "Don't trouble yourself …" But did her brow knit with sudden anxiety?

"No, no, you must see it – did you dust it properly? I saved it from the looters, kept it all these years … in the hope that someone from your family might come – and now you have." She beamed as if she had achieved some prize objective. "It's a precious thing, so auspicious, I wouldn't give it away – though many people begged me for it. Something told me, I knew you would come one day ..."

But Mamma had gone wooden. She wasn't listening any more and actually neither were we – Meena *masi* and I. At least not properly.

"Ah, If only you could take it back for your brother – why didn't he come? Kake … that's what you used to call him, how little he was … He could use it for his son – how many – Oh, don't, please don't …"

It was Meena *masi* who had darted forward. My mother still stood there, as if carved out of wood. Then, as I too started, I heard her wailing … a sound so anguished that it tied my guts into innumerable painful knots.

Yes, it was the cradle. A solid heavy, old-fashioned cradle. Streaks of ancient dust had embedded themselves in the intricately carved wood. But ... in a strange inexplicable way...it still looked remarkably new and unused.

Saida *bua* was clinging to Mamma and wailing too. Then I heard Meena *masi's* voice buzzing in my ears. My eyes were blurring, but I could see that hers were hard and glazed as she said, stroking it over and over again, "I used to rock in it when he wasn't lying inside. I remember ... I remember ... I remember ..."

I grabbed her hand, squeezed it as hard as I could. I had to make her stop. She accused me later of having jabbed her with my nails. I might have. The moment was so charged, so desperate ...

She was humming a tune on the flight back. A tune I knew very well. It was a lullaby my mother had sung to us as babies. It made me feel a little sick now.

"Thank God –" Mamma began when Meena *masi* interrupted her.

"Poor old woman ... do you really believe that the cradle was lucky? I cannot. But you're right. It was a good thing that we were able to keep it from her ... that Kake wasn't alive any more ... That he died before he could get married ... before he could have kids to place in that cradle ..."

"What is lucky or unlucky?" Mamma said, sniffing back her tears. "Who really knows?" Her voice seemed to choke.

But Meena *masi* interrupted. "Are you going to tell *Biji* that we – that I've brought the cradle back? Maybe we'd better not ... I don't know. Anyway, I'm going to keep it ..."

I was the one who gasped aloud. But Mamma made no reply. She just stared at Meena *masi* as if she were seeing her for the first time ... Meena *masi* smiled back faintly ... triumphantly, perhaps.

I wanted to ask her why she had agreed to, or rather insisted on bringing it back, if she really didn't think it was lucky. In spite of Mamma's hesitation, her misgivings. In spite of the trouble, the inconvenience of transporting it. Of course, she had her husband's 'contact', who had smoothed the way.

It hadn't occurred to me that she wanted it for herself. Why? To revive a cherished memory ... or compensate herself for some lingering sense of grievance? Or just to take possession of the new-old cradle which had never been hers ... but which she had wanted so passionately.

And suddenly it struck me that they were right, after all, the old women. For all her strangeness, she had been the lucky one after all. And she had known it ... somehow she had known it, deep inside – the seventh sister. She had known it would be hers ... finally ...

THE CROSSING

The stars still shone out of the navy blue sky when Sandip woke them. Anuradha came awake at once, sensing rather than hearing his call. There was an impulse, electric, urgent, which made her spring out of bed – even though she wasn't fully awake.

"Yes," she muttered, foggily aware of the shape at the window. "I'm awake." Her heart beat unevenly – trying to adjust its rhythm from slumber to sudden wakefulness.

The stars looked bitingly cold, embedded in the dull, cellophane translucence. But she lingered at the window even after Sandip drifted away, seeking out the hill they were going to climb. With its sharp, twisty peak, it was usually quite distinct from the other, more gently moulded hilltops. Right now, though, it looked vague, indefinite, almost a part of the sky.

That's where I'm going, she thought, feeling an acid tingling in her belly.

"Do you want to use the loo first?" Coming out of the dark, Poonam's sleep thickened voice startled her. It sounded oracular, anonymous as a stranger's.

"All right," she said, smiling a little. Poonam hated getting up early, savoured those extra precious minutes in bed. But as she turned, she became painfully aware of a crick in her neck. Irritation spasmed. Of all the days to wake up with a stiff neck!

Clumsy, she crabwalked to the bathroom, sluiced herself with tepid water. She dressed, tugged a comb through her short coarse hair, her body going through the motions like a correctly programmed robot. But her mind kept veering around to the hill – that unreal, improbable destination. On those smooth, soft evenings when they sat outside, faintly curtained by the darkness, a little befuddled by the chilly, over sweet scent of the *raat ki rani*, the lights from that hill had twinkled a secret, alluring message at her. Of a life remote, magical, removed from everything she had ever known and experienced. Of an existence, high, safe and snugly secluded.

So when Sandip had suggested the trek, she'd been the one who'd first cried out, "Yes, let's go there!" her round, normally placid face aglow. Even though she'd never done that sort of thing before.

But she hadn't done this sort of thing before either – walked away from home. Or rather – not returned. Her very presence here was an act of rebellion, open defiance of her mother's wishes. She'd always been a good daughter, eager to please, obey, never rock the boat. So much so, that she often forgot what she had done. So removed was this course of action, so alien to her nature, that she forgot that this wasn't just a holiday visit to a friend. But when she remembered, as she did right now, a tiny needle began to bore into her, deeper and deeper, diffusing a horrible, tingling uncertainty. What had she done? Where was she headed?

Perhaps she hadn't expected it to turn out like this. She'd expected her mother to pursue, threaten or coax her back. Mollify her by announcing an immediate cancellation of the marriage arranged for her, against her wishes – which had provided the provocation. She had hoped that her mother would realise that she was tired of being led by the nose, that she had wishes, desires of her own too.

But, more likely, deep down she'd known that Amma would not follow any such form of action. It was not like her to coax or wheedle. She ordered and people obeyed – particularly Anuradha.

And yet – could anyone react like that? When a daughter whose marriage date has been finalised decides not to return home – acknowledge the event with a hollow, echoing silence? A silence like a still, dark well – that goaded one to throw stones into it, so at least you could see movement, ripples – something at least, disturbing that unnerving depth.

And she had achieved it ultimately. There had been a ripple, a tremendous wave, rather. Maybe she had expected that too, was prepared for it. She had invited it, certainly, with that provocative, challenging letter. The second letter she'd written to her mother.

The first, written from the hostel, probably betrayed her

uncertainty. Made her mother smile, perhaps, after her first fury had abated. So it was possible that that silence was calculated, designed to unhinge her, bring her to heel.

She had been shaken by that silence but not frightened. Angered rather, by the lack of response, of recognition of the fact that she'd left home. As if that silence negated the reality of her action, made it appear as if it hadn't happened at all. As if she did not exist, had no connection with her mother.

How impatiently she had waited for her reply after she left the hostel and went home with Poonam! She had been apprehensive, of course, knowing her. Suppose Amma decided to come and haul her back bodily? What would she do? When it didn't happen, self-recrimination took over. Had she wounded her mother so much, that she was shattered, laid low? She had spent many days wondering if she might even have fallen ill. But as the arid, unresponding days trickled by, silent and inexorable as sand flowing through an hourglass, she had felt confused. A burgeoning knot of pain had replaced the confusion. Was this all it deserved – this momentous decision of hers – and from her own mother? Did she mean so little that she could be totally ignored, her existence erased?

And so she sent that letter which could not, would not be ignored.

"What does it say?" Poonam had asked. She too, had been waiting for the reply, along with Anuradha. Perhaps she had run through the same gamut of emotions, as her thin, taut face revealed – when she took the letter from the postman and handed it to Anuradha.

Anuradha had paled. She had not been able to control the little tremor that shook her hand as she opened the letter. She had felt her face flame as she read it, felt it go hotter and hotter, till the blood rang in her ears.

"I've been disowned," she'd said gaily, through frozen lips, letting it slip from her hands. Her first impulse had been to crumple it, fling it as far as she could. But she had resisted it. Like her mother, she'd decided to minimise her response, swallow the pain in one swift gulp. Poonam's face had stiffened, then creased into lines of sympathy. "Don't worry," she'd said, her slender frame bending forward comfortingly.

Anuradha had shrugged again, though a huge black space was opening up inside, expanding so fast that she was afraid that she'd disintegrate any minute.

And if Varun and Nikki hadn't appeared just then (Poonam's cousins) and suggested a walk down to town, who knows what might have happened. Even now, though it was a whole week since she received the letter, an awful chill numbed her whenever she remembered. In the midst of conversation, she would freeze, conscious that things were different now, she had been abandoned. There was no solid supportive presence behind her. She was all on her own, stumbling off into the dark to some unknown place.

Sometimes an insidious fear slithered over her in the middle of the night, crawling out of her dreams. She'd wake up with a start, shaken by uncontrollable rigors, which would leave her feeling raw, vulnerable as an open wound. And she would lie awake, thinking and thinking, till the darkness dissolved and the hard pale light stung her eyeballs. In a sense, her second letter had been an attempt to reaffirm her connection with her mother. So she had been totally unprepared for that relentless slashing of bonds.

But these moments were becoming rarer. If her mother could be unrelenting, so could she. Because – and at times she could hate herself for it – there was also an exhilaration, an evanescent fluttering. As though she could take off from one of these hills and fly to another at will. Float. Fall free like the wheeling birds that rode the currents all day. Take off confidently, knowing the air, (however unsubstantial it might appear) would hold her up.

The trek had become even more important to her since she received the letter. She could not understand why. But she felt restlessness, almost uncontrollable – urging her on, away from this scene, this place where pain still hung around her, its scent fresh and raw, to the challenge of something new.

"Ready, Anu?" Poonam's voice was nasal, obstructed – as though she had a cold. "I'm getting the food."

"All right." Hurriedly, Anuradha pulled the covers over the bed, tightened her shoelaces, picked up her knapsack and walked out.

Sandip and Nikki and Varun waited outside, looming hazily through the darkness.

"Shall we start?" Without waiting for an answer, Sandip began to trudge up the dirt track that led away from the house –

towards the town – and ultimately the hill.

They followed.

It felt strange, padding off in the wispy darkness. Her knapsack tugged painfully at her neck. But perversely, she nursed that discomfort, would not adjust it to ease the ache. She felt nothing right now. None of the urgency, the need for haste that made Sandip stride so briskly. There was no sense of adventure, no excitement. Only the muzzy feeling, the dullness which was the result of waking up at four thirty in the morning. A kind of disorientation at being on the move when she should have been snug in bed. She felt distant, removed from the others. They seemed alien, strangers – as they trudged along, insulated from each other by the greyness.

Vaguely she took note of Sandip's stocky figure higher up on the slope. He halted briefly, turned to check if they were following, then went on. He had insisted that they leave early so they could complete most of the climb before the sun grew too strong. He was the only experienced trekker among them. Neither Nikki, small, skinny but with a wiry resilience, nor Varun, exuberant, articulate, but oddly silent right now, had trekked that far before. Nor had Poonam. And she, of course, was a complete novice.

She tried to quicken her step, keep a regular pace, in spite of Poonam, who walked erratically beside her. She seemed so wonder- struck at the thought of setting off at this hour, that she had to pause now and again – look around her as if to make sure they were actually on their way.

The house was dimly visible. It appeared somnolent, still with the night. In a different time zone altogether. Because for them the day had already begun.

If I had gone back, Anuradha thought, I would be almost married by now. Almost. She tried to imagine herself in the throes of trousseau collecting – agonising over unstitched blouses, unmatched sandals, purses, cosmetics, jewellery, household apparatus. Floating atop that feverish effervescence a wedding seemed to produce. The centre of it all.

What had made her balk, refuse what she should have accepted calmly – joyfully, rather, as her inevitable fate?

The man's photograph floated up before her eyes – a bland, inoffensive face. Anonymous, a stranger's face. Strange that she should have a stronger recollection of the photograph, rather than the actual person whom she'd met. The grave, perhaps tense young man who had asked her all the expected questions, in a somewhat mechanical manner – as if they had been learned by rote. To which she had given dull, truthful answers, feeling herself thicken by degrees. Turn dense, so dense that she could not respond to the sudden smile that ended the interrogation, which perhaps signalled that a test had been successfully passed.

"No! No!" she had cried out when Amma had smilingly confirmed what she'd suspected. "I can't live with that – that person!" Because that's what he felt like – someone nameless – just a person.

Amma's face had chilled her. "Stop being childish! You have to get married."

Granted, it had appeared to be the perfect match. But she had sensed desperation in her mother's insistence. As if this might be her last chance. As if she were perishable, like a piece of fruit that might rot if left too long on the branch ...

They were walking through the town now – past shuttered shop fronts, through grubby streets where yesterday's garbage festered on the ground. The stench of decay, hung around them, like the dark – faint and cloudy.

Suddenly, street dogs appeared in a clamorous pack. The sound of their barking drummed painfully through the cottony stillness. Varun stooped to fling a stone at them. They retreated – some yelped – though none of them had been hit. They continued to bark, from a safer distance. She was hard put to control the desire to run.

It was a relief to descend into a pine forest again after that. They filed after Sandip, who still marched ahead, important, full of purpose. The leader, who knew the way.

"Isn't it wonderful, being out at this time," Poonam whispered. Her sleep-rumpled face was still ecstatic.

"Yes!" Anuradha began to nod but the crick in her neck stopped her short.

Was it the darkness that made them speak in whispers? As if their voices might disturb someone who still slept? The pines perhaps, who stood around them, wrapped in their private silences. And suddenly she was reminded of her mother again. Would it have been better if she had maintained that silence? Or sent a letter as subdued as a whisper, not one like an outraged yell. At least it would not have led to that break, she thought, feeling the soft pine needles, damp with the morning dew, squishing beneath her feet. But the silence itself implied a break. No, her own action was the break. The silence was merely its consequence. The nothing that remained when bonds were severed.

She had always been aware that a daughter's links are tenuous. And once she left, she could not return. As a guest perhaps, but not with the same freedom, the same sense of belonging. But a daughter who flouted her mother's wishes, what chance did she have--to return, even as a guest?

Still, she had felt the need to fill that silence with something. Even if it were her suppurating grievances. Or had she felt the need to explain, justify her actions?

"... And since I am a burden to you –" (she had written in that letter, the second one). "I have decided to remove myself and carry that weight on my own. Thanks to you (and what a double edged statement that was) I am now capable of doing it. The law recognises my ability to make my own decisions – why can't you? Is it so essential that I tie myself to someone you have picked out, when I don't want it? Are my own wishes so unimportant?" How stilted it sounded – but it was true, so true. She had known she was not being educated for any particular purpose. Only because it was required socially. It also helped to use up that uncomfortable period of time during which a suitable match was being arranged. And it was convenient for her mother that she remain at the hostel, leaving her without the problems a grown up daughter can entail. The constant watching and guarding, keeping her spotless,pure, till she could be passed on to the person to whom she properly belonged. And how neatly everything had fallen into place. Within the last six months that remained for her to complete her M.A., the perfect match had been located and approved of. And actually nothing remained after that but to complete the ceremony which would allow her to dust her hands off. Free of her maternal duties, particularly pressing in Amma's case since her father wasn't there to share the burden.

But she had spoiled it all. No doubt she was already being reviled as an unnatural, thoughtless daughter. Her mother was receiving the sympathy that was her due as the abandoned parent. Perhaps she had been selfish, thought of herself rather than her mother. But why was it demanded of her – that she offer herself up as the sacrifice?

They were out of the forest now, walking down a broadish, paved road that sloped downwards. An incongruity in that remote forest setting. Who could have cobbled that road – and when? It was an ancient piece of work – the stones worn slippery smooth, making descent a tricky business. She could hear the regular, monotonous murmur of flowing water, and she realised that the road sloped down to a river.

The sky had lightened considerably. There was a tea shop close by and Sandip had already stopped there. "We'll have tea here," he called out.

Anuradha slipped off her knapsack. Varun stopped, stretched and yawned, then sat down on the low stone wall that ran along the edge of the road. Poonam fished out the sandwiches they'd brought. They sat there munching, sipping hot tea while the water foamed and tumbled below them.

"The tough part begins now," Sandip said frowning at the river.

Anuradha looked at the hill. It rose sheer and high, straight up from the river. Shrubs and trees crowded its flanks in an untidy jumble. There was nothing of that matt blueness she'd glimpsed day after day. One of the illusions distance created. What would it be like on top, she wondered?

"Okay, let's start," Sandip said, putting his glass down with a pronounced 'ting'.

"Are we supposed to cross the river – like that?" Poonam asked.

"Yes," Nikki nodded. His grin held a hint of malice. "There was a bridge of sorts. I believe it was washed away last year."

Anuradha stared at the narrow plank of wood spanning the gushing rivulet. She felt a harsh chill settle on her. The excitement, the anticipation ebbed, vanished in one swift moment.

"I don't think I can," she heard Poonam say, her voice dwindling in her throat, eaten up by her terror.

Suddenly her own fear seemed to vanish, confronted with Poonam's greater distress."Of course you can," her own voice rang out uncomfortably smug. "It's nothing, nothing at all."

"No – I can't," Poonam quavered. "Isn't there any other way?"

She looked at them again, the rushing river, the narrow plank. Felt a sudden exhilaration.

"No there isn't," Sandip said with dispassionate finality.

She saw the hill again, its lights beckoning. Her longing to go forward was so strong ... blotting out the streaky dawn that grew above the river.

"Come on!" she urged Poonam. She rose, walked down like a sleep walker. She walked down to the river and stepped on to the plank. She could feel that first over springy step. The plank swayed and she felt a nauseous sweat chill her brow, sick and clammy.

She stepped on, her insides molten, shapeless. Suddenly a sliver of sunlight pierced her eyes – unnervingly bright and she felt her foot slide off the plank ... A moment of pure fear, vivid and sudden as a flash of lightning – engulfed her, dimming the cries from the bank behind her as she came down hard – astride the plank. Felt a numb, paralysing terror as she gazed into the water boiling beneath her ... then ... an overpowering urge to succumb, pour herself away into the swift torrent, let it carry her off on its own volition ...

Sandip's voice broke the spell, perhaps. But she had already pulled herself up by the time he had stepped on to the plank to help. Edged her way to solid ground.

A flutter still pulsed in her chest, a memory, a faint remnant of her fear as she sat on the bank, shaking her head at Poonam's anxious queries. She'd come across in a trice – anxiety erasing her terror.

And something like the calm she had felt when she was on the train, en route to Poonam's house, came over her as she gazed at the foaming water, distant now, no longer magnetic, mesmerising. Would Amma have cared if she had succumbed to its allure? What a beautiful revenge it could have been! What a perfect escape!

The impulse seemed infantile now, ridiculous as she glanced away, up at the hill that towered above her. She could see the road, steep, rocky, visible for a short distance – then losing itself among the shrubbage, the sharp scented evergreens.

She thought of the hills behind it, layer upon layer upon layer. If she walked and walked, she could traverse them all, perhaps. And what lay beyond – who knew?

And breathing in the tangy air she thought of Amma – alone, sunk in the well of her exclusion, and knowledge burst upon her. She knew what lay beyond those hills ... She'd find it one day, the way home, find Amma again ... But only ... after she'd traversed all those hills ...

THE BACK VERANDAH

"Do you think Kusum is a nymphomaniac?" Saroj didi asked. Niloo's older sister, a knowledgeable twenty three – her voice crisp and sure with the authority of her college teacher's job.

The words had the bludgeoning resonance of a gong. So strong that it obiliterated Papa's response. Chewing mechanically on her piece of toast, her father's face stretched into a seeming smile, his look of weary patience clearly imprinted, but his voice oddly soundless – twelve year old Niloo considered the words. Nymphomaniac. The exact meaning remained unclear. But not the threatening, almost criminal connotation. Kusum's face materialised in her mind . The over bright, grey-brown eyes, the small, regular teeth, even the lank hair that swung about her chin acquired a faint, somewhat interesting menace.

Confusion followed. The early morning light, pouring in through the skylight turned dazzling. Upset the cool, walled in ambience of the shabby old dining room. Wasn't Kusum a pleasant, no, a fascinating companion? Didn't her mother encourage her to visit their house? And why did she get the feeling that Saroj didi's intent was to provoke, perhaps challenge, that the question was not really a question, but a statement.

Suddenly her father's voice became audible, like an echo returning. She had heard him, of course, but her mind had put it away somewhere, temporarily. "Her father was the same," he said. The response seemed spontaneous, almost a reflex action. Uneasily she realised that in a way he was ratifying Saroj didi's statement. But also deflecting her attack, perhaps. Because, all considered – it was an attack, wasn't it?

Kusum's father. Cadaverous, gap toothed, a fringe of grey-white hair edging his smooth, bald head. Shabby in unpressed pants, shirts that missed buttons. The flavour of the guava jelly she'd smeared so liberally on her toast was unpleasantly strong, suddenly. Could something like that be inherited?

"What is a nymphomaniac?" she asked loudly, to get rid of the taste on her tongue. But repeating the words only seemed to reinforce it.

She heard Papa's suppressed gasp, caught the look of helpless disapproval he threw at Saroj didi. Caught the almost imperceptible shake of his head.He'd forgotten that she was there. Poor Papa. He tried hard – so hard to keep Saroj didi in good humour. It never worked, though and didn't now. She ignored him, keeping her head haughtily averted.

Instead she turned to Niloo."Someone who likes men too

much – in a bad way," she said, slowly, as though weighing her words. With an air of grim martyrdom, as if, however much she hated it, certain things had to be explained to Niloo. She did glance at Papa now. Beneath her lashes – which were long and so extravagantly curling that they were visible, even behind her glasses. They looked out of place in that thin, small featured face, as if they had landed up there by mistake. "A bad girl – or man," she added.

"Now, now," Papa said quickly, clearing his throat. He looked distinctly perturbed. There was a crease between his heavy brows, his long jaw sagged. A sigh burst from him like a whiff of some deep, underlying sadness. "That's not a hundred per cent correct, you know. Kusum isn't really a –." He omitted the words delicately. "She's – well, a little too friendly – maybe." His voice was barely audible.

Niloo's head swung towards Saroj didi on its own. Her face had a faint sneer, a tight, closed up expression, as if she couldn't or wouldn't give any credence to Papa's words. And in a way she would be right, because he had backed up her statement originally – hadn't he? Niloo prepared to edge out of her chair. She didn't like this conversation. There were too many undercurrents, unpleasant ones, she could guess from Papa's face.

"Likes men in a bad way..." What was a good way? Saroj didi and Pratap bhaiya, perhaps. Playing badminton together, chatting on the front verandah. Sort of brotherly and sisterly – after all, his father was an old family friend.

Kusum was an outcaste of sorts, she knew. She'd done

something terrible – eloped with a boy. Strange, it seemed now to Niloo that her father should have gone after her and hauled her back, even as they were preparing to get married. At least, that's what Kusum said.

She'd been properly ostracised after her return. By everyone except Niloo's mother. Ma wasn't there at the breakfast table, right now. She was busy with something in the garden. But Niloo wouldn't have put it past Saroj didi to have said it to her face. She never cared what she said to Ma or Papa. Maybe it was her way of showing that she was grown up, no longer dependent on them. Not that she'd have got any kind of response from their mother. She'd have acted as if Saroj hadn't spoken at all. And Papa wouldn't have replied either in that case.

As she got up from the table, Niloo could imagine the possible scene. Saroj didi fermenting silently, her fine face reddening, her eyelids flapping like an agitated moth's wings behind her glasses.

She had already slipped out of the room when she heard the call, "You haven't finished your toast!" Niloo quickened her step, hurried on to the verandah where the sunlight was spreading itself out, threatening the small geometrical patch of shade that remained.

It pressed against her eyes, making her feel as lethargic as the bees buzzing hazily around the kamini bush outside. Just a few, though there'd be swarms in the evening. The weariness seemed to overcome her, she longed for the cool, scented evening. If only the day could be rubbed out – like a mistake from a copy book-- and evening be written in instead. Then she started, as she heard someone breathe heavily behind her. "Why did you leave the breakfast table without finishing your toast?"

Niloo felt the weight dragging her down but kept her face innocent and bland. "I'd finished eating." She watched Saroj didi's sari pallu swinging behind her, like a pendulum set in motion by her own hurried steps. A green, kota sari, well starched, too nice for just spending the day at home.

"Hunh," she wasn't sure it was an expression of agreement or disapproval. Sometimes she felt Saroj didi was everything a strict mother would have been. As if she felt it was her duty to make up for Ma's tolerance, her ability to absorb the most flagrant misdemeanour calmly. And then it came, "By the way, you shouldn't talk to her so much." Her voice was low, controlled as ever. But – did Niloo sense that same disturbing resonance? "All that giggling and whispering in corners. She isn't your age to be friends with you ... She's not a nice girl, Niloo."

Niloo turned. Saroj didi's face was expressionless, her eyes did not censure. It was not as if she was blaming Niloo. Just telling her what the right thing was. But Niloo felt embarrassed, she didn't know why. As if by association something of Kusum had rubbed off onto her.There was also a faint, uneasy flare of rebellion. Ma never said anything, why did she have to interfere?

I will, I will, she repeated to herself as she ran out, letting the summer sun smite her face. It had a harsh, clean force unlike Saroj didi's words which seemed to quiver and dart as if not quite sure what they wanted to hit, destroy ... And then it came to her – why didn't she call Kusum, Kusum didi. She was much older than her – eighteen to be exact. Was it because of her diminished social status? Did that particular act – or whatever tendencies she possessed; tendencies that could justify Saroj didi's epithet--bring her down to Niloo's level?

Not that the ostracism seemed to bother her too much. Niloo had heard the story of her elopement, narrated like the account of a trip to the movies. Told without shame as her mother sat in the verandah entertaining an acquaintance.

Ma had been sitting on a round backed cane chair. Mrs. Prasad faced her on its matching counterpart. Cups of tea, chocolate biscuits – Niloo had been munching on one – stood on a table between them. Kusum sat on a moorah, embroidering a table cloth. She had a fine hand for such work and Ma encouraged her, getting cloth and threads for her to work with. Actually she had been doing this kind of work for Ma before she took off. She'd been a B.A. student then. After that her studies had come to an end. Her father had a good excuse not to send her back to college. No one had bothered to offer her any chocolate biscuits. Not even Niloo. She wanted to, suffered as she munched a biscuit. It felt dry, stuck to her palate, but her hand felt too heavy and weak to pick up the plate and pass it to Kusum. Or maybe it was her mind.

Actually, Kusum hadn't volunteered the information. It was Mrs. Prasad who asked her, in a hoarse, accusing sort of a voice,"So where all have you been roaming, hunh? ... How could you think of doing such a thing? Aren't you ashamed of yourself?"

Niloo had noticed the way her mouth had pursed when she arrived, knitting bag in hand and saw Kusum sitting there, head bent over her sewing. "So, you've put her to work?" she'd remarked, with a look full of malice. Ma had nodded in a bored, indifferent sort of a way. As if Kusum's presence there was as unremarkable as the maid, Kalyani's, picking wheat a little distance away. Not something which was an unforgivable social blunder in a small town. Where someone like Kusum was not forgiven easily.

Kusum had given a literal reply. Deliberately, Niloo suspected. She'd laughed, causing Mrs. Prasad to start. "I wanted to – we-we wanted to ..." her head snapped up, her pale eyes glinting at Mrs. Prasad, looking her full in the face. She giggled shamelessly. " I crept out at twelve thirty. I'd flung two changes into a bag and hidden it – I didn't want anyone getting suspicious." She had smiled in a conspiratorial way as if making them all party to her adventure. Mrs. Prasad had frowned, but perhaps her curiosity had prevented her from protesting. "It was pitch dark," Kusum went on. "Rakesh, like a fool, hadn't even brought a torch. We tripped and rolled down the hill as we were running off."

She'd giggled uncontrollably as she said this. Her shoulders loosened, the table cloth slipped off her lap. Mrs. Prasad had made a choking sound. Her sari pallu had slipped off her shoulder too. It often did – exposing a large expanse of cleavage. Niloo never missed an opportunity to get a good eyeful. There was something fascinating about that deep crevice. As if it held some enticing mystery within it.

But right now even she had felt outraged at Kusum's audacity at reducing something so shameful into a joke. But beneath that outrage there was a sickening excitement. She could see them rolling down the hill, their bodies touching, piling up on a heap upon each other... She'd glanced up at her mother quickly, wanting her to censure, admonish Kusum. But her mother sat there, impassive. Her mouth had twitched faintly. Was she suppressing a smile or an impulse to scold Kusum? Niloo had felt let down, diminished in front of that cat Mrs. Prasad, who would no doubt spread the story all over town.

Even Kalyani had snorted. Kusum's smile had lost its brassy glaze then, become a little fixed as if she didn't know what to do with it. She, too, had glanced at Ma. In an appealing sort of way, as if asking for some kind of support. But Ma had merely looked abstracted, lost in distant thought.

Mrs. Prasad, on the other hand, had clicked her knitting needles venomously and said, "*Besharam*! You should be ashamed to show your face. Anyone else would have drowned themselves instead of going about all plastered with powder, dressed up to kill. How does your mother allow it?"

She had glared at Niloo's mother who'd jerked back to life, murmuring something vague like, "She's just a young girl ..." hurriedly picking up her tea cup and gulping the cold dregs that remained.

Kusum's face had flamed. She'd opened her mouth to speak, then she'd glanced at Niloo's mother and stopped as if she'd received some hidden message. After a long, breathless moment she'd got up instead and whispered to Niloo, "Come. Let's play cards."

Niloo had gone reluctantly. She'd found Mrs. Prasad's outburst as annoying as Ma's failure to put Kusum in her place. She was not quite sure whether it was something she could accept, the fact that Ma had appointed herself Kusum's champion. She couldn't speak out against it openly – like Saroj didi, who seldom lost a chance. Specially when everyone else had barred their doors to her. Did it mean that Ma condoned Kusum's behaviour? Surely she didn't. Was it just plain bravery – standing up for someone, whom everybody condemned? And that was one thing she was very unsure about. Ma's bravery. Could someone as silent and passive as her be considered brave? Or was it something in the same line as sending the sweeper's children to school, passing on old clothes and leftover food? And Kusum – did she really deserve or need that kind of support?

"*Churail,haramzadi,*" Kusum said as she shuffled the cards clumsily.

"Kusum!" Niloo cried out severely, "If you abuse in front of me, I'll tell Ma." Even though she felt a liberating excitement gush up inside her. There was something so wonderfully devil-may-care about words like these. "And ... You're dropping all the cards." She was still chafing at the fact that she'd been compelled to range herself on Kusum's side in front of Mrs. Prasad. But she didn't have the heart to reject that appeal –which it certainly was. Because – and this was something that made her really uncomfortable at times, she couldn't help liking Kusum.

"I'll tell Ma," Kusum had mimicked, her face blackening... "No, no, don't get annoyed. Can't I joke once in a while?"

Niloo had jerked her head away, torn between fury and fascination. She'd pounced on her cards and frowned at them avoiding Kusum's glittering, mesmerising eyes. Her pale, taut, thinlipped-face. But a few minutes later she'd been rolling in her chair as Kusum reproduced Mrs. Prasad's tone of voice with cruel perfection. She'd even run into the dining room silently and brought the whole tin of chocolate biscuits, which they'd devoured with gusto.

So what, if she isn't my age, she thought now, running towards the back verandah. It would be cool and shady there, flanked as it was by two large trees, bordered with numerous overgrown bushes. A place where Saroj didi never went. She'd encountered a snake there once, she said. Niloo would be safe. Safe to sit and think.

But, as she approached, she heard voices. Two of them. Kusum's and another – a man's voice.

Niloo halted, overcome by curiosity as well as a vague dread. The man's voice was low, just a murmur. Kusum's laugh rang out shrill and metallic, though. It sounded different, somehow. It made her uneasy. Churned something up inside her, set little prickles of sensation zipping down her skin. Zipping, prickling – all gathering together to accumulate in that one particular spot between her legs ...

Breathless, she wondered, biting down on her lower lip, letting those feelings ripple up and down her in pleasurable waves...what was Kusum doing there so early today? She normally arrived in the afternoon, stayed on till the evening. And the man, who was he?

She edged forward, trying to keep her breath even. Then stopped. Did she want to see who it was? Suppose, suppose they were doing something... Something she oughtn't to see? She felt a tight, stuffy fullness in her chest ... Then a sudden, tearing hatred for Kusum. Nymphomaniac. The words surfaced, knocked against her head. Nymphomaniac, she hissed, feeling as venomous as the snake that had frightened Saroj didi. Tearfully desperate, she tiptoed ahead.

Kusum's laugh rang out again – the man's followed – in an awful complementary sort of a way. Was there some kind of a sound – a sort of shuffling, scuffling? But already Niloo could feel her skin harden around her, set like an icy case. She had recognised the laugh. It was Pratap, Pratap bhaiya, she should say. She shouldn't have gone further, she knew, but she couldn't stop herself. She wanted to be sure – absolutely sure. And just as she stepped forward, the lizard appeared. Darted out from nowhere – across her path, almost touching her foot.

After that she was conscious only of the shrieks filling her ears and Kusum and Pratap bhaiya's frightened faces. Kusum's eyes unreal, like a stuffed tiger's, bulging from their kaajaled outline. The minute beads of sweat on her upper lip. So close she could have counted them. And – she could not help noticing that her chunni was missing, the buttons of her kurta open, exposing that dark, deep cleft, making her want to reach out and put her hand inside. As if that would solve the mystery, eventually. And Pratap bhaiya ... he looked strange too, his nostrils dilating, his chest moving up and down as his breath came out in little panting gulps ... as though something inside him was expanding, expanding ... and would explode any minute.

Then she began to laugh, helplessly, uncontrollably. "It was nothing, nothing," she said. "Just *a girgatang*. I got scared ... uh – where did you all come from?" Easing her arm out of Pratap bhaiya's hard, warm grip. It rested too close against the side of her chest, too close to her tiny bosom.

He turned his head and mumbled something. Kusum remained silent, tightlipped. She really puts too much powder, Niloo thought. It stood out whitely on her wheatish skin. She didn't look pretty any more.

"If you're looking for Saroj didi, she's inside," she told Pratap bhaiya, who nodded vigorously and turned towards the house.

"You've come very early," she flung at Kusum, who shrugged jerkily but still didn't reply.

Half an hour later, though, Niloo found her perched quite placidly on her moorah on the verandah . God knows what happened to Pratap bhaiya. Neither he nor Saroj didi were anywhere around. "What's this now?" Niloo asked, looking at the new piece Kusum was working on.

"A bedcover," she said, without looking up.

"A bedcover ... for whom?" She knew very well for whom, she asked just to keep the conversation going.

"For your sister's dowry," Kusum said. She looked up now.

And laughed. An ugly laugh, like a piece of cloth ripping.

"Her dowry?" Niloo exclaimed. "But she's not getting married." This statement too, was superfluous, she knew. Her sister's dowry had no connection with a marriage date being fixed. It was being, had been in the process of preparation for quite some time, in spite of Saroj didi's protests, her scorn for such things.

"She's hoping to, I expect," Kusum laughed again. She bit off the thread with a vicious jerk.

Niloo felt the hatred rear up again. She squeezed it down, carefully. "And what about you," she said insinuatingly. "Aren't you hoping to get married too? Why aren't you preparing your own dowry?"

Kusum's face darkened. "I would have been married by now," she said. "If it hadn't been for my stupid father!" Niloo was shocked at the throb in her voice. "I would have been far away ..." She sniffed, the pale eyes filled up, spilled over ...

Niloo didn't know what to say. Was she expected to console her, because she hadn't been able to do something everyone said was wrong, horribly wrong? Confusion swept over her again. Maybe it was that confusion that made her ask, in a soft, confidential tone, "What were you doing back there ...?"

Kusum stared at her, her eyes like marbles. Her lips were beginning to draw back from her teeth when Niloo, panicking, whispered, "Are you really a nymphomaniac?"

The moment she said it she knew she'd done something unbelievably, irretrievably foolish. Disastrous in fact. Something perhaps a child half her age might have better sense not to do. But it was all their fault, she thought later. Saroj didi's and Papa's and Ma's and Pratap bhaiya's and of course, Kusum's. Most of all Kusum's. For being one.

She would never forget how Kusum repeated it, though. "N-nymphomaniac ...?" her thin, dark lipsticked mouth expanding and hissing as perhaps a snake's might. "Who – who said it? Tell me – who said it?" Her pale eyes held Niloo's frightened ones so close that she felt the moment of understanding shoot through her, like a bolt of electricity consuming both of them. A sob burst out, large and so plangent that Ma heard it and came out. To receive the rest of Kusum's fury.

Yes, Niloo would never forget it – the bedcover coming flying at Ma, like a sail torn from its moorings. "Let her make it herself, her wretched trousseau – if anyone will ever agree to marry her ..." And as Ma stared at her astounded, "Whatever I may be, I'm better than her! My parents were married at least ..."

Ma swayed, she might have fallen, Niloo rushed forward to catch her, but she righted herself. "Kusum, Kusum, child, what's the matter?" she said weakly. Her arms reached out after Kusum, who was already stomping off. They dropped helplessly then. She sagged into a chair, her eyes closed, her body limp.

"Ma! Ma!" Niloo cried, overcome by an appalling guilt and an even more terrifying fear. "Can I get you a glass of water?"

She ran off without waiting for a reply, but not before she'd come face to face with Saroj didi and Pratap. Saroj didi's eyes were enormous behind her glasses, her mouth was working.

Pratap managed to look baffled and guilty at the same time.

It was later...much later. Kusum had left, fled – no not fled – she'd stomped off, leaving a trail of invective behind her. The same words she'd used for Mrs. Prasad. They made Niloo feel sick, loathsome now. Niloo stood at the door of her mother's room. She wanted to go in there, say something, but she didn't know what... how...And when she heard Saroj didi's voice, she halted, of course... "Now he knows – thanks to her. How could you let her into the house--how did she know? Does everybody in this town know--that I –?" Her voice had crumpled up after that. Lost that unassailable confidence, which was so much a part of her that Niloo couldn't imagine her without it. "I-I thought you'd come here because – How could you do it?" Her voice jerking out, an acid, hurtful, spray, showering Ma with hateful words. She'd heard the sound of stifled weeping and Ma's anguished reply.

"Sssh-ssh, beti. Don't say that! Don't ever say that!"

Niloo stood outside, shaking. She could see Ma's tears falling too, silently, ceaselessly, even though there was a door between them. Sometimes one can see through walls. She had felt a pain in her belly so sharp and acute, that she doubled up and almost screamed.

Of course, Kusum never came again. In fact, she never went anywhere. Like Mrs. Prasad and many others wanted. Niloo wondered if it was a kind of justice when she caught a glimpse of her outside her house as she passed that way once. Her belly grotesquely swollen, her clothes shabby and careless, her face plain and lifeless, bereft of make up. But it also filled her with a terrible fear. Because suddenly, Kusum's face vanished and another superimposed itself ... And she found herself running, running, till she realised it was futile. After all, she had to go home.

Probably Saroj didi had been seized with a similar impulse. She had run, too. Taken up a job in a college in a big city. Ma had been silent, impassive as ever. Papa was the one who'd looked broken. "I always considered you my own child," he'd whispered, when Saroj didi was leaving. But she'd said nothing. The only time she showed emotion was when she hugged Niloo.

Niloo might not have recognised her but for those extra bright eyes. A hefty, overdressed matron, with two children in tow. She had quickly suppressed the thought that had sprung up on its own...which one ?

She'd reached out to embrace Niloo, who had been trying to turn away, with enthusiasm. She'd been stiff in that embrace with the remnants of that old ambivalence haunting her. And of course, the scar of that old memory, which had changed so much for her. Too much.

But Kusum wouldn't let go. She rambled on – as if all that had never happened. As if they were really old friends meeting after a long time. Maybe she wanted to remember it like that. But then the moment had come. She had asked softly, "How's your sister?"

After Niloo'd replied, told her about Saroj didi's successful, meaningful life, she'd said with a sigh, " I wanted to come and meet your mother so many times ... But –" she'd looked Niloo in the face with an anxious, no, a desperate insistence, "I never told anyone. Tell your mother – I never told anyone ... It's such an odd thing ..." her face became still and thoughtful. "Rakesh – the fellow with whom I ran away –" here she giggled in the old careless way. "His sister told me. We were staying with her when – you know, when." Her smile had been wry, but good humoured. "She'd known your mother a long time back. When it happened, before she met your father and came to live in this town."

Niloo felt the old shame rear up, wrap her around like a scaly skin. She had not told Kusum that they didn't have much part in Saroj didi's life. None of them, certainly not Ma, or bewildered, well meaning Papa. Niloo, perhaps. But not enough.

She tried to conjure up the old hatred, but couldn't. Odd she thought, time can eat up hatred, but shame is indigestible.

But not for Kusum, perhaps, because after she moved away, she heard the old coquettish laugh ring out. She half turned her head, unable to resist the curious impulse and saw the broad back, the grey head of a middle aged man ... And she could see those pale eyes glinting. She felt the old confusion again as Saroj didi's epithet surfaced. Was she right in a way? Small comfort, she thought, considering the price she'd paid, they'd all paid, for her naivete, her need to show off and – her need to get even with Ma.

THE JEWELLED SERPENT

After the rains are over and the sun shines hot and hard, slowly, surely, the green grass shrivels. The long juicy strands turn brown as they bake steadily in the afternoon sun. Wild flowers lose their colour, die slow deaths on the hillsides. The caressing monsoon mists dissipate and the mornings turn blindingly clear, the sky brilliantly blue, the sun's beams cutting through the air with sharp insistence, as they decimate the rainbow sheen of the dew drops. Bake the moist ground pitilessly till it's parched, coated with powdery dust.

But in the evening, the breeze turns balmy, captivates with an intoxication that has to be felt to be believed. And sometimes, after the darkness enfolds the hillside like an impatient lover who cannot wait but rushes madly to enfold her beloved, a strange light is observed, moving along the ground.

The lucky ones see it and hold their breath, count their

blessings on fingers that have suddenly turned rigid, paralysed with the knowledge, the sheer terror and delight of a potent spell invading their lives. Seal their lips because good fortune is as ephemeral as the monsoon mist and luck broadcast is luck lost. So they guard the magic, swallow it quickly so it's safe in their bellies, working silently, secretly to transform their lives.

But what is this vision, yearned for by so many but granted only to a few?

It's the snake, the serpent of serpents, the legendary *nag* with a *mani* in its head, the jewel that shines as bright as the luck it vouchsafes.

But, there are also some who are indiscreet, profligate with their luck.

Like Vasundhara.

Nandi was with her that evening, standing under the cold green shade of the deodar tree. Vasundhara, who with her cropped hair and tight fitting jeans was somehow alien to the small hill town, despite the kinship she insisted on when she took possession of the old house with its vast retinue of pines.

"What's that?" she'd cried out. "Down near that bush. Something burning ... A cigarette butt?"

Manoj, one the group that gathered around Vasundhara, captivated by the allure of the big city girl, was the first to respond. He had enough presence of mind to dissemble, casting the allure aside (after all, each emotion has its parameters and why should an outsider discover a local treasure?), "It's an electric wire sparking, probably."

"But ... it's moving, it's moving ... " Her breathless tone told Nandi she knew. "Could – could it be what Mamma told me ... the-the mani nag?" A little embarrassed, fearful, as she turned to look at the faces that had suddenly closed up.

Nandi felt a sudden hatred uncoil. How long had she wooed the *mani nag*! Laid out saucers of milk, waited in the smoky dusk for its coming till her eyes ached with weariness. She needed that luck desperately, to escape, get away from the old man. The shrivelled old man, brittle as the dry grass, who had bought her youth, possessed and guarded it like a dog in the manger. Her youth, charged, potent as the hot rays of the October sun, which was wasting itself, night after throbbing night. The chorus of the crickets outside as endless and maddening as her bondage. Helplessly pressed against the prickly ropes of her string bed, her nipples as sharp and hard as nails, longing for a fiery shaft to consume her, as she listened to the old man's ragged snoring, his coughing, his farts.

How badly she needed that luck! So much more than this privileged, foolish girl.

She peered into the darkness desperately, but the light had gone. The trees loomed, the crickets chirped, monotonously repeating themselves like the days, weeks months, years of her life. The life that stood still while the seasons changed. The old man grew older, true, slid closer towards death. But so did she. Panic brushed her as she saw herself shrivelling like the grass, turning into a dry and sterile husk.

God knows what made her linger after the others left, even

though it was long past the old man's dinner time and she would have to suffer for it. Hope that the *mani nag* would return?

"Maybe ... you'll get married now ..." she told Vasundhara grudgingly. Because Vasundhara, told her once, about her mother's eagerness to see her settled. And her own.

"Get married? Would that mean getting lucky ..." The seemingly innocent eyes suddenly turned sharp and shrewd, "Would it?"

The words direct as an arrow, more piercing because it found its mark. "What would then?" she snapped.

"What would ... love? Someone giving themselves up, surrendering to you totally. That's luck."

Nandi almost laughed. How naïve this city girl was, how much in the grip of movie magic. Could a man ever surrender ... totally?

But as she stumbled down the rocky path, feeling the thorns tearing at her, not bothering to avoid them, she knew she was equally naïve. Secretly, didn't she dream of that, even though she knew it was impossible? Someone coming into her life, rescuing her from the old man ...

It was Nandi who saw the stranger first, leaning against the wall of the hillside, puffing on a *bidi*. It was the *bidi* that confused her, then his eyes. They had a greenish, phospherent glint. Like-like the light of the *mani nag* might be, she thought, crazy with excitement. His body was sinuous and compact, his face leathery yet young, despite the tired lines around his mouth.

She could not move, it was as if invisible rays paralysed her, forced her to stop and gaze fearfully into his eyes. He was an outsider, not of her class, despite the *bidi*. But ... was there something special developing in his glance? She turned dizzy, willing it to escalate.

But Vasundhara, Vasundhara again! She broke the spell. The blunderer, who thought impossible thoughts, her narrow face still glowing faintly with the remains of the luck, a mere shadow of it. She herself had frittered away the substance.

"Are you looking for someone?" she asked with more than a touch of asperity. Vasundhara who treasured, fiercely guarded this space. "This is private property." Trespasser herself, warning off the other who had unknowingly wandered here.

The man smiled. A slow deliberate smile. Even Nandi could see he meant to charm. There was calculation in that smile. She was not sure whether to hate him or gloat over what might be Vasundhara's downfall, even though she had usurped the *mani nag*. She was a fellow female after all and Nandi knew the man spelt danger. She could smell it on him. Her nose had become attuned to such smells, living with the old man. It made others think her fair prey. As much as she could smell Vasundhara's innocence despite that fund of irrelevant knowledge she claimed to possess.

"I'm sorry," she heard him say softly. "I didn't know. It's beautiful, do you live here?"

She could feel the air around her melting as Vasundhara replied, suddenly hesitant, unsure, "Yes ... no ... not permanently."

Nandi had to move away. She had caught the senseless, dazed look in Vasundhara's eyes. The satisfied smile that wiped away the tired lines from the stranger's face. They barely noticed her going.

Love? Surrender? A faint shadow of pain overlaid Nandi's heart. For herself or for Vasundhara, she little knew. The darkness came down with a slow reluctance as the murmur of voices behind her teased her ears. She almost sank down on the path, willing the relief of tears, but knew it was no use.

Was there any relief for those for whom time had frozen?

For Vasundhara it seemed to race or spin like a dizzy top. A motion that scattered, disarrayed the customary routine of their lives.

Vasundhara roamed the hillside with the stranger, while the mani nag still hid itself, ignoring her saucers of milk. One evening when she was coming down from the temple, her desperation driving her to pray and pray as if she could pray herself out of this morass, she saw them. The stranger's body was coiled around Vasundhara's, pressing her into the ground.

She wanted to tear them apart that day.

When would Vasundhara discover he was the *mani nag's* curse? For throwing away, scattering its gift to the wind? Strange that at the temple a prayer for Vasundhara had slipped out. A prayer for innocence, a prayer for knowledge. A prayer for freedom, a prayer for bondage. But ... whose freedom, whose bondage?

Then one evening, a voyeur's sick longing drew her to Vasundhara's place, after a long, long time.

She found her alone.

"Nandi ..." she said. "You haven't been coming."

"You had company."

Vasundhara laughed. "Not any longer ..." Nandi did not know how to fill that aching silence. But Vasundhara did, "He could not surrender himself ... neither could I."

Nandi could see the tears course down Vasundhara's face, even though she did not turn her head, feel them rather on her own face. Remembering her prayer for freedom.

The saucers of milk are dry. Perhaps a cat has drunk them. Nandi has not been keeping watch. She knows the *mani nag* will come on it own, if it comes at all. But ... she's not sure ... if she wants it to come at all ...

VISITORS' HOUR

The hands of the little clock on her desk have crept past the five thirty mark but Nitya hasn't noticed it. It's the announcements on the public address system that alert her to the fact that it's visitors' hour. A misnomer actually, because visiting time at the girls' hostel stretches on till eight thirty for male guests (women can visit throughout the day). Then it's time for dinner and the chowkidar shoos out all those who linger with the air of righteous superiority his authority endows him with. Out of the stuffy rectangular lobby where visitors perch on scuffed rexine settees, examining the boards on which the names of the former office bearers of the hostel are painted, while they wait. It's mostly parents or other elderly relatives who occupy these seats, with impatience or fortitude according to their respective temperaments. Boy friends tend to stand around like eager, chafing horses or stroll up and down on the straggly patches of grass outside.

The announcements reach her ears like scratchy music from a distant loudspeaker, a sound that her brain registers but does not consider worth deciphering. Her eyes remain glued to her book and her mind is a resolute wall shutting all distractions out. The assignment has to be handed in tomorrow and twenty-two-year-old Nitya is serious about her work. And then she knows there's no chance of her getting any visitors. She is a local and there would be no occasion for her mother or brother to visit even if they had the time. Mamma is not the type to go in for frivolous stuff like surprise visits and her younger brother Akshay who might be inclined to once in a while, is too busy cramming for his board exams, apart from the coaching and tuitions he has to take to be a worthy competitor for the various entrance tests which will follow. The magic keys to the enchanted world of success, on the door of which they have been knocking long and hard.

In any case she goes home almost every other weekend. She hates to admit it, but apart from the desire to bond with Mamma and Akshay it is a despicable weakness that is another powerful draw. Her mother's cooking. She hates the hostel food, the discomfort of cramped accommodation, of having to share common toilets and so on and has long dithered between the options of living at home or the hostel. But it's not just that she would have to travel a long distance to college each day. There's something about the neutral, detached world of the hostel that makes her feel at peace despite the inconveniences that come attached as a necessary corollary. There's a certain unidentifiable stability in this dispassionately regulated way of life. She had used the excuse that she can study better to move here. Maybe it's true. And possibly too, some instinct has prompted her to use this experience as an introduction, a breaking in process for the final break which will come soon – when she leaves home to create her own life. She knows it will be quite different from the one she has led so far.

But both Mamma's cooking and Mamma have become more erratic than ever. There are days when she is effusive and loving, serving up all her favourite dishes, leading Akshay to exclaim, the last time she had done it, "Hey, you better not miss a single week-end, Didi. At least I get some decent food for a change."

She had swallowed the gasp that had whooshed up her throat, thrown a quick apprehensive glance at Mamma. But instead of flaring up as she had feared, she had laughed, ruffled Akshay's hair, probably because she knew he hated it, and said, "I better give you some bad food for a change, so you have real reason to complain."

Nitya's busy writing away in her notebook when the door is pushed open roughly. It's her roommate Rachna, who'd gone to pick up some snacks from the canteen. She can't study, she says, without something to munch upon. Her angular face is furrowed with irritation. "Have you gone deaf?" she complains. "They've been announcing your name for the last ten minutes."

"Announcing my name?" Nitya's full soft mouth hangs open.

"Don't look so surprised. You've got a visitor."

Something in the way Rachna says this fills Nitya with unease. But she knows it won't be any use asking Rachna to explain. She takes a perverse delight in posing riddles, not providing answers till you're so exasperated that you're not sure you want to know any longer. The only way to end the suspense is to go down as fast as she can and find out who it is herself.

She runs down the pitted gray cement stairs without even bothering to comb her disheveled hair or change her faded T-shirt, doesn't even pause to think that at home Mamma would never have let her appear before a visitor like that. At the entrance to the lobby she halts for a moment to examine the bunched up groups deep in conversation. But she can't see anyone she knows. Could Rachna have been mistaken? Only when she hears her name being called out does she recognize the familiar voice. Her breath catches, reluctantly her eyes swivel around to clash with his.

It's the toupee that has confused her. She should have experienced revulsion, disgust but feels nothing but embarrassment that she couldn't recognize her father, even though it's been a while since she's seen him. Self-castigation follows and then a wry amusement. It's in keeping with the persona that he has assumed, ever since he left them, this startlingly younger looking man whom she has known as her father. A kept man needs to pay attention to his appearance and maybe he doesn't need to maintain the façade of dignified authority a father with grown up children has to, perhaps, any longer.

Despite herself she can't help exclaiming, "Papa!" Then glancing around to see if anyone's watching.

His sheepish smile makes crows' feet fork out on his temples, making him look old again. He comes forward briskly to mask the awkwardness, but something quivers at the corner of his mouth. She forces herself to think of Mamma – her brittle laugh, the chain smoking, the time she found her sitting all alone in the drawing room staring at nothing when she got up to get a glass of water at night, but it doesn't work. That barrier crumbles, inexplicably. There's a tearful gratitude in the way she allows herself to be embraced (later she's going to hate herself for it) inhaling the familiar scents – his cologne, the harsh odour of his tweed coat. A new one she notes, withdrawing. His girl friend treats him well, she thinks, and the unbidden thought causes something to close up, clamp her chest with chilly bands of steel. The fleeting moment of joy flees along with her smile.

But he doesn't seem to notice. It's enough perhaps that she has received him without obvious animosity. "What's happened to your contact lenses? Why are you looking such a studious type? And so thin too. Doesn't your – " He stops himself in time, covers up by saying, "Don't they feed you here?"

Her smile returns, much diminished, though. "When did you come?" she asks instead of answering. Maybe such questions are just rhetorical. He doesn't live in Delhi any more and this is only the third time she has met him since he left two years ago. Sneaked out of the house to go and live with his rich girl friend.

Funny, she thinks, in a way it was a relief when he actually left. Not that there were scenes, quarrels, any ugliness between her parents before that. But unlike Akshay she had been able to sense something deep and hidden behind those silences. Something more than the common or garden displeasure that had caused her parents to stop talking to each other for days on end earlier. Or had she really? Perhaps all she been aware of was the discomfort that that plangent disquieting silence had caused her and instinctively blamed him for it. And that in itself perhaps had opened her ears to the whispering, the meaningful glances neighbours and relatives had targeted them with.

How long had those silences existed? She wasn't too sure. Mamma had always been quiet, he was the one for words. Strangely, though, Mamma had opened up after he left, had become almost verbose, as if someone should fill the empty space he had left with sound.

He answers the question she is not inclined to ask, not out of fear of unpleasantness but inexperience of such meetings. She does not have any friends who have estranged fathers. Her quick, keen eyes have not had the opportunity to observe the niceties of such social encounters. Perhaps she should have used this opportunity to punish him, as he deserves, hand out the tongue lashing which is his due. But like Mamma she hates loud voices, angry words and would rather sacrifice the pleasure of putting him down than face that unpleasantness. "I came here for some work and couldn't leave Delhi without seeing you at least," he says.

"Do you hate him?" Rachna had asked. It was one of those nights, when lying awake in the stuffy little room, proximity, the darkness and the stillness of the night had coaxed them to let those hidden thoughts flow, thoughts which they hid so assiduously in the light of day. When both she and Rachna seemed different persons, so confident, so much in command of themselves. So seductive was the allure of letting everything flow out in that dimness that many a time she had had to exert all her will power to rein in those runaway thoughts.

All the same, she had answered Rachna truthfully, as she stared at the faint outline of the fan whirring above her, as if it would help to make that dilemma clear in her mind. "It's funny, but I don't."

Rachna's reply, "That's strange, but you're a very tolerant person," filled her with unease.

No, I don't, she tells herself again looking at the short blunt nose she has inherited from him along with the full mouth. Perhaps it's because suddenly she's not so sure. "Don't you want to see Akshay too?" she hears herself ask. It's a natural response to his statement. If he can't leave Delhi without seeing her, it's natural that the same sentiment would apply for her brother. Mamma wouldn't mind she knows, but she's not too sure if Akshay wouldn't. His anger is enormous, such a huge swelling wave that sometimes it threatens to engulf them all, and he has never made any attempt to hide it, even if it were possible for him to do so. Being a girl, or perhaps just being practical by nature, she has learned to stopper emotions which create nothing but frustration, lead to pain greater than the initial agony, even though this kind of capitulation sometimes fills her with shame.

"Do you need anything?" he asks.

"Not really," she wants to reply. Mamma's job pays reasonably well, their needs are few and simple, and they are definitely not in want. But with a shock she discovers a strange greed forking up. Greed so strong and overwhelming that she cannot control it. She shrugs, smiles piteously and glances away. "Oh...no,not really..."

He rises to the bait and quickly counts out three thousand rupees from a wad he produces from his pocket and stuffs it into her hand with guilty haste. The notes feel stiff and harsh against her palm and crackle faintly as her fingers close over them. She does not have a purse in which she can place them so she lets her taut hand fall clumsily into her lap.

"Is it enough?" he asks, anxious lines etch themselves on his face.

She nods with an artificial, awkward smile, notes the way his eyes cloud.

To her astonishment he quickly counts out four more five hundred-rupee notes. Her palm feels stuffed to bursting now.

"Have fun," he says, stretching his mouth as far as it can go. "This is the time to enjoy life."

She can only nod, confounded.

"Is Akshay studying hard for his exams?"

"Yes, Mamma's made him join coaching classes. I'm sure he'll do well. He's determined to." She prattles on. "I'm going to be through this semester. I've already got placement. In a firm in Mumbai. Mamma thinks I ought to get married but I want to concentrate on my career right now. I think it's more important. Don't you?"

She pauses to glance at him. He hasn't responded with more

questions but is examining the grimy floor intently. Perhaps he hadn't bargained for so much information. Perhaps he's not really interested in her-their plans. He's wearing nice shoes, she notices, suede, a sort of grayish brown. His clothes are definitely more stylish now. Maybe – she, his girl friend likes him to dress well, buys him clothes. Mamma didn't really care.

He startles her by saying suddenly. "Your mother's right. Get married. You can have a career alongside too. She managed quite well didn't she?" Then pales and stops abruptly as the import of his words strikes him.

Mamma managed quite well. Too well perhaps. Did it make it easier to leave her knowing she was such a good manager?

"How's your new wife?" She should ask Papa perhaps. It might be impolite if she didn't but she can only take her old name, the name they had known her with when she was the friendly neighbour who liked to spend time at their place. The jolly middle-aged lady with brightly hennaed hair who made such good samosas, such excellent biryani. So lively despite the fact that she was a widow with an only son who lived abroad leaving her all alone. All alone with so much money that she was desperate to find someone to share it with her. Funny she found someone who lived so close by but had to move so far away with him. What had won him over, the good cooking, the readiness to exchange jokes – or was it something else?

"How's Mrs. Nath?" she finally asks with neutral courtesy, not sure why she is.

Papa, cool customer that he is, replies, "She's fine…she likes to call herself Mrs. Chopra now." There's something comically conspiratorial about his smile and an insane giggle escapes her. For a few minutes they both laugh hysterically.

She stops short when she sees Rachna passing by. She looks disapproving. But later it makes her laugh even more for some reason. Perhaps it's the odd sense of superiority that sweeps over her. Rachna doesn't have a father who's run off with another woman and now wears a toupee and natty suede shoes and hands over five thousand rupees to his daughter to have fun with, without turning a hair. Not everyone can dare so much.

"Yes," Papa repeats. "She likes to call herself Mrs. Chopra now." He winks as if they share a secret." She tries to giggle again but she's all laughed out and the sound she produces grates on her ear. "Maybe she'd like it if you would call her Mummy."

She turns rigid and even he realizes he's gone too far. She can hear his heavy breathing despite the sounds of conversation all around her. Ordinary normal conversation. Ordinary normal people. Not fathers who run off with other women to live as kept men and begin to wear toupees and stylish suede shoes but gray haired or bald fathers who count the costs of their children's education and balance it with the salaries they will expect to earn later, while planning for their impending retirement alongside.

"I'll send you more money, whenever you need it." She's about to protest when she sees him expand, throw her a knowing glance. "I've taken up a new assignment," he says. "They pay very well…I'd like to send Akshay abroad to study – only… I'm afraid your mother wouldn't agree."

She stares at him for a while before answering. "Why shouldn't she? She's not the type to stand in our way – you know that!"

"Yes I know that," he repeats shamefacedly then lets out a small, wispy sigh.

She feels an odd prickling underneath the thick sleeves of her cardigan. It's so sharp that she can't move, is compelled to sit frozen to her seat lest it become unbearable. She can barely hear him say, "All right, Nitu. I'll be seeing you more often. My new job means I have to come regularly to Delhi ... Take care." He stands up, then bends to kiss her on the top of her head. She doesn't turn to look as he walks away or wave good-bye but simply moves on stiffly towards the stairs that'll take her back to her narrow room and the assignment that seems like a weary burden now instead of a stepping-stone to a magical new existence.

Only the shout from a girl behind her, "Hey, you're dropping your money!" alerts her to the fact that her fist has opened up and the crumpled notes are scudding across the dusty floor like precious wasted hours. She turns to nod her thanks and hurriedly scoops them up.

She's not quite sure how she will spend this money, as she is not sure what it means to her.

If she were to consult Rachna what would she say? You should have thrown it back on his face, or out of the window, or donated it all to charity?

She knows she wouldn't do any of these things. Because a

stubborn belief wedges her in, she has a right to it even if she's not sure if she believed him when he said he had a job. Let Mrs. Nath – who wants to be known as Mrs. Chopra, even dares to imagine them calling her 'Mummy' now, pay. Pay for her fun and Akshay's education abroad. It's the least she can do.

WHY DID YOU KILL MAHATMA GANDHI?

Possibilities are endless – and thought a river ever flowing. But reality is inescapable to. And therein lies the rub.

Ms. Lal looked at the grass, the green of the trees outside. A tiny, creeping excitement bubbled and bloated inside her. The leaves were so unbelievably green. So unnatural, a miracle in this city of dust and grime.

As if someone had been up and about, cleaning, polishing them especially for her. Yes, there was something to be said in favour of sickness. Everything looked new, different. She hadn't felt so alive, so charged with energy for ages. Now she felt clean, new and whole, ready to take on anything. Cleaning cupboards, cooking an extra-special meal – starting on that exercise schedule, so essential and yet so often postponed. They all felt like extraordinarily exciting things to do! And of course, how could she forget, buying material for new sofa covers. She wrinkled her nose, (rather short, a little broad but quite attractive, all the same) as she looked at the grubby, discoloured shapes before her. Receptacles for people to lower their backsides into. To recline, lounge, sit upright, or perch nervously at the edge. Or wipe their greasy fingers on, nonchalantly, indifferently, furtively, overcome with pangs of guilt, perhaps. She would make them fresh and new like herself, make everything fresh and new in her life.

And then, as unexpectedly, dissatisfaction clamped itself on her. A damp, fat wave, an irritable mist blotting up her ebullience. Trust her to think of sofa covers instead of letting that wonderful, rare exhilaration carry her off to something different and momentous. Something that could transform her from this shapeless lump in the not so new sari with toenails that needed to be trimmed, somewhat like one of the sofas opposite her, into someone quite different.

Not someone who just cleaned cupboards and cooked extra special meals and for whom an exercise schedule was something revolutionary. She saw herself opening up like Chinese boxes and a series of Monisha Lals emerging for her to pick which one she wanted to be. Yes, she could even choose to be a mini-skirted person with purple hair, someone who would not nod benignly and just tap her foot when music played but would dance, dance, dance with wild abandon. Whoorf! It made her breathless just to think about it. But, as always happened, spoilsport reality interposed and she saw the Chinese boxes closing in on themselves and shutting up, confining the dancer, the adventurer, the buccaneering entrepreneur – all those possibilities – deep within that crevice inside her, that magical cave, where they'd always lived.

How rooted one got! How impossible it was to take flight! Sometimes she felt small, incipient wings beating inside her, watching TV programmes with people going off to exotic destinations, setting off on dangerous expeditions, braving discomfort, bug bites, bad food, going without bed-tea and proper meals– (*dal, subzi* and *roti* for her). How do people manage without the kind of food they're used to? How ever! She couldn't stand visiting relatives even, where the tea didn't taste like what she was used to, the *rotis* were not cooked to the right consistency and the pillows didn't feel the same. She could never get a decent night's sleep away from home. But all the same she longed to be able to dash, zoom off at a moment's notice, arrive at some impossible destination with a happy face and a smile for the camera. And here she was ... such a firm fixture, such a well-fitting round peg in a round, permanent hole, made to measure for people like her.

The saddest fact was, no one could ever dream that she could even harbour such fancies. Worse, surely no one could believe or imagine that she had ever been young – a frolicsome, lively child even. In fact, she'd almost forgotten it herself.

A little girl in a frilly frock and a ribbon in her hair. Quite a cute child if you looked at her childhood photographs. Black and white, of course, sometimes a little out of focus. But still one could make out that she had been a pleasant looking child.

She remembered her older brother's friend. What was his name? It had escaped her—permanently, perhaps. She couldn't even recall his face. Odd, he was always at their house. Only the peculiar question he used to ask her – "Why did you kill Mahatma Gandhi?"

What a thing to ask a six year old child! But it was one of those quirky, nonsensical things boys liked to do, to tease, provoke and build up a crazy exasperation in someone younger. Someone easy to scare and confuse.

She remembered her frantic denial. The sickness, the terror squeezing her belly. The feeling of guilt, irrational, though it was, lodged in her like a speck of grit in her eye, which couldn't, wouldn't be blinked out even though she wept streams of tears.

"No! No! I didn't!" she would cry, her voice going higher and higher.

"Yes, you did," he'd whisper. "I know you did, admit it." His eyes would fix her, round, glassy, accusing. She'd tremble, her lower lip curling like a baby's, unable to control herself.

"No-no!" she'd mutter, beginning to whimper. Her mind raced ahead contemplating all the horrible possibilities. She could see the police coming, the handcuffs, the bars of the cell and ... the noose.

At six she had been aware of these possibilities. She even knew who Mahatma Gandhi was, guessed at the heinousness of the crime ascribed to her.

"No!" she'd scream. Their laughter saved her temporarily. Danger, terror, became a joke as she stared at their faces, all flashing teeth, bulging cheeks and crinkled eyes. She felt bewildered at first, then the speck in her eye melted away. Or did it entirely? A tiny atom remained. The seed of fear, almost invisible. So did a kind of perverse self-importance. She, Monisha, little Monu, as they called her – all of six years old – had been thought capable of killing Mahatma Gandhi. A big, important man, whose picture was everywhere. The absurdity of it all did cast a film of doubt, cloud that importance. But – they had said it, hadn't they?

And that accusation, so outrageous, so disproportionate, hummed in her mind, filling her with quasi murderous intent, making her scare her little brother by yelling, "I'll kill you!" Play at throttling him till he screamed in turn and her mother came to separate them.

"What's wrong with this girl?" she had said. "Has she gone mad?" That had opened up another line of thought. She was no longer a possible murderous but a mad little Monu. And being mad gave you some kind of license, she knew.

It wasn't a good thing to be mad. But certain activities did require a kind of madness. Had she really possessed it once, or had she just imagined she had? It was hard to be sure. She had never explored that possibility enough.

But there was one thing she was sure of. No one would dream of asking her now, "Why did you kill Mahatma Gandhi?" And she knew she should be thankful for it, because it would definitely imply some modicum of insanity in the questioner or a taste for particularly sick jokes.

They could only ask, "What's for dinner?" or "Why hasn't the maid removed this cobweb?" Or "Where should we go this vacation?"

And if she replied, "Boating down the Amazon," her husband would probably smile and say, "Sure let's – what a wonderful idea." But just a few minutes later he would continue without even changing his expression, "If we have to go to Goa this winter, we must make the bookings now."

And her own mind would work itself into a frenzy, computing costs, air fare, hotel stay, transport, meals and want to abandon the whole project in despair, thinking of all that money being blown up, their nest egg depleted, her bastion of security weakened. And she'd say, "Need we go that far? Won't it be better to go somewhere closer? Bharatpur for instance?"

Her husband would look relieved and say, "Yes, why not? That's a better idea. I really can't get away for long."

And she'd relax too. And yet remain dissatisfied. As if she'd tightened another knot. A knot of safety securing her safely within herself – or a noose, slowly tightening around her neck, not letting her breathe. Not letting her gulp in huge mouthfuls of invigorating, energising oxygen, which might even enthuse her to actually attempt all those extraordinary things she could only dare to dream about. But as she sank deeper and deeper into the morass of middle age, shut her eyes to the allure of the rain forest, the squawking birds, the stealthy, dangerous beasts, abandoned the chance to be a weather- beaten woman in jeans (broad beamed but tough as they come) who braved the piranha infested waters of the Amazon or the snowy, impossible heights of the Himalayas.

Well, this was life, she thought rather droopily – suddenly no longer inclined to clean cupboards, begin an exercise schedule. What for? She was not a young bride who had to prove her housekeeping skills to her in-laws, she was not even interested in being slim and desirable any longer. It was not appropriate now – not even worth the trouble. Yes, that was another thing denied to her now. She could not dare to try and look attractive. She would not be able to face the mockery of her peers – the over ripe ladies she met at kitty parties, mechanically playing tambola or munching *samosas* with avid greed, the gimlet eyes assessing the value of her jewellery or the diamond ear rings she had acquired not out of any great desire for them but as a necessary adjunct to her station in life.

But the grass, the grass, the shiny waving leaves outside! They remained so exotically verdant. It was real, that extra special brilliant green, that bright, impossible dimension.

She wanted to feel, experience that gloss, that colour, that freshness from close. Remembering how she used to lie, roll, in the grass, inhale its sweet scent from close, chew upon a juicy stem. She had climbed trees too. She could remember the hard scabby trunks, the branches, the exhilaration of being high up above the ground. If only she could become a bird perched on a tree surrounded by nothing but leaves. If only ... she could float off, free herself from these lumpy anchors, the heavy shapeless sofas weighing her down, rooting her to the earth ...

But I'm too heavy, she thought. The branches will snap ... there's no tree that can hold me up now ...

But they didn't ... though the leaves were not so green from close. It was not that comfortable either. The wood bit into her behind, there were ants. A spider swung perilously close to her nose. "Shoo! Shoo!" she cried, batting it with her hand. As if it could hear. Could it? Could spiders hear, understand human talk? Would it understand if she shouted out, "*I* killed Mahatma Gandhi! *I* killed Mahatma Gandhi!"

Of course, she hadn't killed Mahatma Gandhi. The spider knew. But she didn't know, hadn't been sure, the day he had come upon her alone. He hadn't been laughing then. His eyes had been round and glassy as ever and his voice had hissed in her ear. "I know it. I know you killed Mahatma Gandhi."

"N-no," she had stammered. "I-I didn't." She was utterly bewildered. She had thought that chapter closed. Several days had passed since that incident, though at times her older brother did tease her sometimes, saying, "Why did you kill Mahatma Gandhi?"

"I didn't, I didn't," she would reply, mechanically playing along, but not disturbed.

But today she was. More than disturbed. Fear had crawled up her arms and taken possession of her heart. It had banged and thumped at her from there, making her lips stiff, her mouth dry, her breath short as he clambered up the tree to sit next to her.

"Yes – you did ..." He had fixed her with his gaze. Try as she might she could not pull her eyes away. When he said, "You will have to be punished ..." it was almost a relief. She would do anything to escape that nameless, creeping terror. If she expiated, the guilt would be cancelled ... if the guilt could be cancelled, the terror would go away ... That's why she didn't mind it at all. Didn't mind that hand coming down, hot and hard against her bare behind, didn't mind what followed either ...

The cool green leaves had suddenly been spattered with mud. As if the unknown somebody who had been polishing them for her had decided to muddy them again in a fit of perversity.

Funny she couldn't remember his face or his name. He had left the town soon after when his father was transferred to another place. She had been thankful. Her terror on beholding him had become a joke, though, for her brother. She had fled whenever she caught sight of him from afar. She did not want to be punished again. Because the guilt hadn't gone, not the terror. She had never been quite sure that she hadn't killed Mahatma Gandhi ...

HOUSE OF CARDS

She always lost, yet she continued to play. Why? She often asked herself. True, it sometimes gave her a kick to see his hard-earned money go down the drain. But there were times when she felt an unutterable, unbearable sadness overtake her – that she was so unlucky – even in cards. But the sadness strangely enough was as satisfying as the kick of pleasure. Maybe because it was like an automatic, built in punishment for her wickedness, cancelling it out, leaving her with a clean slate, a blank page in her copybook to blot all over again. What a worthless woman you are, she would tell herself, losing all your husband's hard-earned money. (Actually she was not hundred per cent sure if it was really hard-earned, but it felt better to tell herself so. It honed the edge of the razor of guilt with which she loved to lacerate herself, drawing blood in the form of tears). Often she went home and cried. Sometimes she couldn't even wait that long and like a junkie desperate for her fix, began to cry in the car itself as she drove home – it made her feel better much sooner. Sometimes if the tears were reluctant to come she actively encouraged them to. She would deliberately focus her thoughts on her empty purse and his anger when she asked him for more money and told him that she had lost again. She would also think about her compliance that night when he put her through the routine. The days she lost she could actually enjoy it, while on normal days it brought on a horrible nausea.

Sometimes she got the feeling that he too got a kick out of her losing. That no matter how much he berated her, told her she was a worthless woman, no good for anything, it gave him some kind of satisfaction. As if her losses brought on some deep, inexplicable excitement. They definitely did. Didn't she know! He always coughed up, never refused to give her any more money, never told her to stop playing and he really enjoyed punishing her. She wasn't sure if she could stop playing but he never gave her the opportunity to find out. She didn't want to think about this too much. It confused her, diluted the feelings of guilt that were so important to her.

The day it happened – her adventure – that's what she liked to call it, she was really crying badly. She had lost a lot so the tears burst out the moment she left Minnie's house. Minnie's house was particularly unlucky for her. She always lost like mad even though she really loved Minnie's house, she'd done it up so well. Just the way she would have done up her own house if Rajat let her have the money. Funny, he never liked to spend too much money on the house, always said he was short when she wanted to redecorate. Anyway, she was barely able to restrain herself, didn't even wait to tuck into the wonderful spread Minnie had laid out. Minnie always did everything very well. She even won most of the time, small reasonable sums, not extravagant amounts, which would have aroused envy and led to grumpy mutterings from people and snide remarks that she cheated.

She simply dashed out of Minnie's house, almost tripping over her trailing *dupatta*, desperately sniffing back the tears, scrabbling in her purse for the car keys, which seemed to have got hidden in some inaccessible corner as usual. Her tears almost blinded her as she started the car and began to drive down the road.

It was one of those dim winter evenings and people had already turned on their headlights. So foggy and smoky that she didn't bother to roll up the window. She felt absolutely sure that no one would notice the tears flowing down her cheeks in extravagant streams. She would have a headache by the time she got home, she knew. The thought gave her a dull satisfaction.

She had to stop at a red light. She was weeping really piteously by now and feeling absolutely wonderful about it, when a sudden impulse made her fling a quick sideways glance to her left. That sudden prickle of consciousness, that recognition of another presence that tells you that you're being watched, had overcome her. Sure enough she was. It embarrassed her a little. But by this time she was too far gone to stop. She couldn't, her tears had an energy, a life of their own, they were beyond her control. So she looked straight ahead and continued to cry and feel the man continuing to watch her as if fascinated by this orgy of weeping. It was as if they were sharing something at that moment. She wasn't sure what but there was a communication of sorts. Then she thought she heard him say something. The words were indistinct and she wasn't even sure that she was imagining it all. In any case the lights changed just then and the cars behind her began to honk and she had to move on, half thankfully, half regretfully, because she was a little curious about what he was saying to her. A little confused too. He looked sympathetic, she thought. But she wasn't sure whether to feel happy or sad about it or whether it was good or bad that a strange man waiting at a traffic light next to her should react to her tears.

It's nice when someone looks sympathetic, of course. But when you've done something bad then it's not good at all she knew. How can one sympathise with a wrong doer? You need to punish them and she definitely deserved to be punished that day. Not only had she lost heavily again but she had also left her poor little baby with the maid the whole day. The baby she was supposed to love and cherish but somehow didn't feel like a lot of the time.

All she wanted was the heady excitement of the card table and one enormous, mind-bending jackpot of a win. So she could take back a huge wad of notes and fan Rajat's face with it – or better still, strew them on the bed, pull off all her clothes and roll in them naked. Feel the sharp, crisp notes against her soft body ... And then ... and then ... she would jump on him the way he jumped on her ...

Yes, she was bad, bad, really perverted ...

And to crown it all, now she was pulling over to the side of the road because she had noticed that the car had been keeping close behind her.

Was the man following her? Would he stop? Would he ask her why she was crying? This was being impossibly bad, but she really wanted all this to happen. But it was worth being bad so you could feel good when you were punished for it later on.

Sure enough, the car behind her stopped. And as she waited in the semi darkness, shivering, staring into her mirror, she saw a man get out and walk over. The footsteps rang deafeningly loud in her ear in spite of the clamour of numerous impatient horns blaring. Or was it her heart beating?

Her chest went so tight as he approached that she felt she was about to explode, to burst into a thousand million fragments. "Any problems ma'am?" he asked, leaning down to gaze at her through the half open glass. His voice was as warm and soothing as toffee on your tongue. "I was a little concerned. I could see that you were upset."

A stranger ... concerned about her! That made her cry even more. But she wasn't sure whether it was good or bad. It was good to be sad, she knew, but she wasn't crying because she was sad. She was crying because his voice was so warm, so kind.

His stopping, stopping for her, felt so good. As good as the sense of guilt that surged up when she remembered that she'd stopped deliberately. Just to see if he'd stop too.

When he spoke again his voice sounded alarmed – as if that torrential outpouring was not what he had bargained for. "What – what's the matter?" he blurted out.

She said the first thing that came into her head. "I'm sad."

The man was silent for a moment. He had expected something more specific perhaps. Some tangible reason for grief, which would help him to offer a solution. But she felt it was an honest, straightforward answer. She *was* crying because she was sad. "Anything I can do to help?" he asked uncertainly.

"Yes, make me happy," she wanted to say, though the thought made her laugh inside. The sheer insanity of asking this poor good-hearted soul to make her happy. And maybe she did. Maybe a small giggle did escape her, because she noticed the way he started. But all she actually said was, "Thank you, thank you," sniffing into a disintegrating lump of tissue.

He peered at her uncertainly through the darkness as if not knowing how to continue. In a way he was trapped. Having stopped he could not just walk off even though already she could sense a kind of impatience with himself for getting into such an uncomfortable situation and with her for not giving him something substantial to work upon.

"I'll be all right, thank you so much," she found herself saying again, her voice surprisingly steady now even though a sinking disappointment was taking hold of her.

The man would walk away, relieved. She would carry on home. The tears would keep on flowing till she had expended all her sadness, emptied herself of guilt and grief.

She would go home and tell Rajat that she had lost again. He would lose his temper, she'd bear it stoically – then the grand finale of her punishment. Though it was becoming more and more mechanically ritualistic – her wrongdoing – his anger – the punishment. A keen disappointment lanced her. She might as well as not have stopped at all if this was all that was going to happen.

"Thank you, thank you," she repeated again softly, because the man still stood there as if uncertain about what to do.

"Would you-would you like a cup of coffee or something?" he asked hesitantly.

A cup of coffee! Now that would be something really bad. Having a cup of coffee with a stranger. She experienced a heady tingling, felt her whole body clench into a knot of excitement. "O-okay," she sniffed. As if to show him that it was just the remedy for all her sadness ...

Walking into the coffee shop of a five star hotel, she felt exposed, naked in the bright light. She had thought of them going to a cosy, dimly lit place. He seemed to sense his mistake too, because he made an impatient sound.

"Is this-is this place okay?" he asked, looking into her eyes. He had rather nice eyes, warm and bright. In fact he was rather nice altogether. She had gotten lucky for a change. "Actually – I'm staying here ... " His voice trailed away, as if there was something he wanted to say but could not for some reason.

She said it for him. "Maybe ... maybe we could go there – to your room – it would be more private. You know – just in case –" Just in case I start crying again was what she meant to say.

The sudden glint in his eye spoilt it all, the quickening of his breath. It showed that it was just not mere kindness that had led him to stop. Would he have stopped for an ugly woman?

Or did it really? She felt confused. What did she really want from this stranger? If it was sympathy, which made her feel temporarily good, but guilty in the long run because she was bad, she didn't deserve sympathy, kindness. Punishment, expiation, these were things she understood better. But maybe in some twisted way he was doing her a kindness. Giving her an opportunity to be bad so she would deserve her punishment more. The punishment Rajat would definitely mete out when she got home late. She felt her own breath catch at the prospect. What a tremendous castigation it would be!

Funny how one got used to being hauled over the coals. How it became an essential part of one's life. Almost as necessary as breathing or eating. She thought of the punishments she had received in school as a child ...

She had been sent to boarding school at the age of five, when her mother died. The memory of her first punishment remained vivid in her mind. She had knocked over a glass of water at the dining table. The standard punishment for this was a caning administered after dinner. She remembered the sick apprehension in the pit of her stomach. The horrible wait, the painful expectancy. The longing, longing for the moment to arrive so it could be over. The desperate wishing that some magic would make it vanish altogether. That sister would have a sudden change of heart would forgive her, would hug her and say it was inconsequential, a minor fault which could be overlooked.

Of course that didn't happen. And she could clearly recall

the hard, tingling feel of the cane coming down on her hand. The sharp whiplash of pain, which stung tears from her eyes. And the relief ... the blessed relief when it was all over ... and she could retreat into herself rubbing her aching hand. Be thankful that her wickedness had been cancelled out. The slate was wiped clean ... and ... she could sin again.

She sinned often in many ways during the course of her school life. Perhaps they appeared to be petty misdemeanours when she thought of them now. At the time they were considered outrageous crimes. Like dancing in the rain, eating wild berries or playing noughts and crosses in class. As she grew older her wrongdoing became more heinous – like trying to jump over the school wall to go and see a movie, writing a letter to a boy etc. etc. It was not that she did it deliberately. It just seemed to happen on its own. She only discovered that she had erred when someone pointed it out to her. Maybe she was just born to be bad. It was in her genes perhaps. But then, there was something she felt pretty smug about. She never shirked her punishment. She paid for whatever she did. And that made it all right.

Later, when she passed out from school, Dad took over the responsibility of punishing her from the nuns. And the first time he did it, it was horribly painful too. The same sharp, piercing pain, like the cane coming down on her hand. No, a hundred times sharper and more painful. It was not a pain that could be smoothed away by time like the caning. There was the bleeding and the excruciating consciousness that this act was irrevocable. And then there was confusion. Because instead of cancelling it out, the punishment brought on more guilt. An enormous, unbearable load of it. It was also hard for her to pinpoint her offence. Sometimes she felt she was being punished for no reason at all, just for existing, maybe. And perhaps that was reason enough for Dad. She was thankful at least to be able to do something that seemed to give him some kind of satisfaction. But she was not too sure about that even. Because he invariably wept when it was all over. He even begged her forgiveness at times. That made her cry too. Worse, it made the punishment seems less of one. Because aren't the righteous meant to chastise the wicked?

"Why are you sad?" he asked, looking at her curiously with those warm bright eyes. They were sitting in his room. A typical, pleasantly decorated characterless hotel room. Perhaps just the right setting for this bizarre interlude. He had ordered coffee from room service for her and poured out a drink for himself.

"I'm sad ... because I'm bad," she said. Then giggled because of the silly rhyme it made.

He laughed too, thinking it was a joke. "But seriously," he asked. "Why were you crying?"

"Because I lost in cards ... I'm always losing in cards ... Squandering my husband's hard earned money ... "

He stared at her for a moment with those lovely, serious, honey brown eyes. "Then why don't you stop playing?"

"I can't. Don't you see? I can't!"

"I'm sure you can if you really want to." He looked really earnest when he said that. She felt like smiling. How innocent he was. As if life were that simple!

"I'm not sure that I want to ... "

"Then why cry?" he looked exasperated now.

She was silent for a moment. Then, feeling that he deserved an explanation because he had, after all, made a serious effort to help her, even if there might be some ulterior motives involved, she said, " I like to play cards. In fact I'm crazy about it. But I always end up losing as I told you ... and then I hate myself."

"And your husband – what does he say?"

"He gets angry! He punishes me. But he always lets me have the money."

"Punishes you? How does he punish you?"

She dropped sugar cubes into her coffee, stirred them, felt them dissolve in the liquid. Like the heat of punishment dissolved her guilt, absorbed it. She looked up at him, ran her tongue over her lips. "He has ways," she said with a suggestive smile and giggled.

Bright sparks shot out of his eyes, scorched her. He gazed at her for an endless moment. She felt herself melting, liquefying inwardly. "Shall I – shall I punish you today?" he asked, his voice hoarse.

That made her think. Why should he, a total stranger, punish her? How had she wronged him that he should mete out chastisement? Punishment had to be earned ... But then ... how had she wronged Dad? And he had punished her all the same ... How he had punished her. He had only stopped when Rajat took over.

"All right," she said. "Go ahead. Punish me ... "

She couldn't even wait, began to undress right away, she was that impatient. Because a sudden unbearable excitement surged up within her. Rajat would have even more reason to penalise her tonight. This – this was probably worse than playing cards. Much, much worse. What a stroke of luck, finding this man!

Her mobile trilled even as the last shudders of bliss were dying away. "Coming, just coming, darling," she murmured, as smooth as honey in the face of Rajat's anger. It promised so much!

Tonight would be the mother of all punishments ...

THE FOLLOWER

The bazaar is still the same. More crowded perhaps, more bodies jostling for space, newer and better merchandise perhaps, scattered in the same state of disarray in the shops. The smells are the same. The syrupy odour from the halwai's shop, mingled with the reek of heating oil and the fragrance of the rose essence used to flavour the sweets. The overpowering odour of asafoetida at the bania's shop, a veritable bully among smells which will not allow any other a chance to express itself. The tangy odour of freshly plucked guavas from a vendor's cart, the tart scent of oranges which made you long to reach out and suck one, feel the clean, tingling juice trickle down your throat and clear your head of all those other oppressive odours. How much could Lalitpur change?

Vasudha was not sure what had led her here. Even though it is something not done, to go out of the house, roam around in the market till all the rituals that follow a death in the family are complete; she had been unable to tolerate Buaji's prying questions, her sister-in-law Archana's fussy attention and Vikram's sullen eyes any longer. So she slipped out quietly when she thought no one would notice she'd gone.

Perhaps it was the desire to connect with Prateek, so strong at the back of her mind that she'd dreamt of him accompanying her here last night. The thought of it made her wince. What was her subterranean mind cooking up? She had left for Lalitpur in such a hurry that she had been unable to call and inform him that Babuji'd passed away and she was going home for the funeral. She had not forgotten, actually. But at that vulnerable time, she had felt unable to cope with the probability of his wife picking up the phone. Early in that relationship she had laid out certain parameters for herself and always maintained a scrupulous taboo against calling him at his home. As if extra marital affairs had their rules too and their code of conduct like everything else. But now that she was here, looking for an STD booth (she had experienced an odd reluctance about calling him from home, too many walls with ears) she realized that the disinclination went deeper than was obvious to her. She knew she'd sound distant, disoriented, causing him anxiety. It might be better to let him discover the news from her office. She'd make her explanations later, when she was back in Delhi, in more secure territory. Surely he, the psychiatrist will understand, with his expertise in matters of the mind, of its odd and inexplicable aberrations?

The moment she decides, the place suddenly begins to crowd in on her and she's overcome by an urge to go back, crawl into the dim, quiet spaces of her parental home, away from this scene of chaos.

She's turning to look for a rickshaw, already framing her responses to the questions, the admonitions she should expect to face, when something surfaces. Not in a flash, but a slow creeping realisation, the unwanted stench of a long suppressed memory identifying itself.

This is the same place, where she'd come upon Rajni's follower that time. The recollection still sends a shiver through her. She might not even have noticed him in the crowded bazaar, amidst the jumble of bodies, the reaching arms, the clamouring mouths, if it hadn't been for the whiteness of his sling. It had flashed at her from amidst that motley mass. And the sling led her to his face: swollen, misshapen, mashed like an ill-treated melon. Even though she'd known what had happened to him, she could not keep herself from starting. His bitter eyes met hers that very instant, flared at her accusingly ... she hadn't been able to help feeling the razor of culpability slice her through and through.

It had begun harmlessly enough ...

The cycle rickshaw bumps over ruts, labours up the slight slope towards the bazaar. It trings noisily past cycles and hand carts if the rickshawala is young and energetic. Rajni and she sit clutching their books, eyes demurely cast down. They look neither left nor right, conscious of invisible blinkers. They talk in low voices, their frequent bouts of laughter are gagged the moment they spill out, with balled up handkerchiefs or hidden behind the ends of their chunnis. It's impossible to contain their laughter. It has a way of spurting out, unbidden. Almost anything can set it off. They shake silently, grow purple with the effort of holding it in. But still it will erupt.

They know very well that laughter is dangerous. It's non-serious, frivolous. It even carries a hint of moral laxity. Good girls don't laugh aloud, they stretch their mouths sweetly behind their chunnis. Worst of all, it's an invitation to the wolf – whistling roadside Romeos who lie in wait. An encouragement to spew out the comments that they have to encounter each day – being girls and they being boys. They have to pretend to be impervious to these assaults – blind, deaf, dumb. They turn wooden or rather metallic, do not flinch or move a muscle when those kissing noises rake the back of their necks like a blunt edged saw. They try to pretend that those grinning faces are part of the scenery – like the sulphurous stench of the drains that pursues them most of the way or the rich, green odour of rot that foretells the approach of the vegetable market.

That's why she's surprised when Rajni nudges her one day and says, stuffing her giggle back into her mouth with her chunni, "There he is again!"

"Where?"

"Behind us in the checked shirt, silly!"

She had allowed her head to swivel around slowly with an elaborate pretence of casualness. Yes, there was a checked shirt atop a scooter. A thickish neck grew out of it and a somewhat coarse featured but oddly attractive face with a dense mass of hair on top of it. He's moving slowly, keeping pace with the rickshaw.

"Who's he?"

Rajni shrugs, tosses her curls back carelessly. "How do I know? He follows us every day." Her face acquires a frightening magenta tinge as she tries to choke back another giggle.

"Why?"

"Silly!"

Of course, it is stupid to ask. Any six-year-old kid could have told her, and she is all of seventeen. It's romance! Romance that manages to blossom even in this dusty town, with all its stringent taboos. She feels a shiver ripple up her back, feels a tingling that energises each and every pore of her being. But then the inevitable question rears up, a huge wet sheet slapping down her excitement – who is he following? Rajni or her?

It is soon answered. Because Rajni begins to undergo a kind of metamorphosis. Like the cold winter winds, she too is melting, softening as the days pass. As the mango blossoms thicken on the trees in pale clusters and the heat gathers strength. Her kaajal grows darker, her curls float languorously on her cheeks. She even begins to sport dangly ear-rings.

Vasudha hadn't liked it – her appropriating the Follower. Perhaps he was hers from the start, but it made her feel as if she had lost in a game or failed in some kind of test. She longed to imitate, outdo her, snatch him away, but did not dare. Amma's eagle eyes were all pervasive. Sooner or later she would surely notice what was going on. And she could not dare to contemplate the consequences.

So the Follower begins to irritate her. She wishes he would

desist, miss a day, fall ill, break a leg, but he's as regular as the clock in the tower that looms up in the middle of the town keeping time for all of them. He turns bolder. Sometimes he whizzes past, whistling or humming a bar from a hit film. Sometimes he'll turn ostensibly to yell out a remark to a friend behind him. But actually to gaze boldly, familiarly at Rajni, making her wriggle on the seat.

And one day, he grows so bold as to throw a note into the rickshaw. It falls on the floor between them. For a moment both of them ignore it, pretend it isn't there.

Then Vasudha says through lips that have suddenly turned stiff, "Pick it up, Rajni."

Trying to suppress the acid burning within her. Corroding their friendship.

Rajni giggles. Caught up in her dream world she has been completely oblivious to the turmoil raging within Vasudha's breast. She opens the note, flushes and giggles again, balls it up in her fist.

"What does it say?" Vasudha's unable to resist the question.

Rajni shakes her head. "Secret," she laughs, her black eyes glittering. Excluded, Vasudha's left to nurse her resentment. But she was sure Rajni would have told her, sooner or later, if things hadn't suddenly taken such an unexpected turn.

Later that day, as she lies gripped by the drugged and feverish sleep that seizes one on summer afternoons, she has a strange dream. She's going off alone in a rickshaw to some unknown destination, when she sees the Follower come up behind her.

"Hurry!" she calls out to the rickshawala in a panic. "Don't let him catch up!" But though the man pedals with all his might, the Follower is coming closer and closer. So close that she can feel his breath hot on her neck. His laugh rings out evilly as he pulls her chunni off. She's screaming, struggling ... and then, inexplicably she finds herself spread-eagled beneath him, his face floating above hers, his hand hot between her legs ... She wakes up sweating, gasping, flushed with an unspeakable shame ...

She finds it hard to meet Rajni's eyes the next morning, though she is extra chatty. But something changes that day. The Follower doesn't turn up. Rajni's restlessness grows as they traverse the long stretch of the bazaar, almost reach their college. Her mouth droops lower and lower, she's almost beside herself with disappointment. Vasudha herself is gripped by an uncontrollable sense of uneasiness even though what she has wished for has come true. Is it guilt for ill-wishing her friend that makes her long to glance back, like Rajni, to see if the familiar figure has appeared? The same guilt that compels her to desist, fearing it'll add to Rajni's misery. She fervently hopes it might work as a kind of charm; that the Follower might make a miraculous reappearance if she doesn't turn her poisoned gaze in his direction.

The next day it's worse. Rajni keeps turning back, again and again. Only to confront a vacuum. She's so distraught that she doesn't even bother to conceal her anxiety. Vasudha longs to offer some kind of consolation. But doesn't know what to say, isn't sure how it will be accepted.

The mystery is solved that very evening.

She's at her desk studying. The old table fan is spinning behind her, recycling hot air. Vikram appears suddenly at the door.

He stares down at her for a moment, the inevitable frown dividing his thick brows, clears his throat, then mutters, "By the way, that fellow won't pester you any more. I've fixed him. *S-sala, harami*!"

She gazes at him baffled, peers questioningly into his red-laced eyes. They have a peculiar gloss, it makes her blench. "Who, Bhai, no one's been troubling me?"

"Arre, that idiot who used to follow your rickshaw. Rakesh told me. *Badmash*! We've settled him good and proper."

The book she's holding slides away from her hand, the pages rippling agitatedly, like so many dry leaves being stirred up by a unexpectedly violent gust of wind, as it falls to the ground and bangs itself shut. A legion of ants crawls up her spine.

What would she say to Rajni? That her silly little romance has been brutally ended by Vasudha's over solicitous brother, intent on preserving his sister's honour?

Poor Vikram, she thinks with a sigh, what a task he had set for himself. He had blundered right in the beginning and to this day he had not been able to achieve that goal. Little had he reckoned with what he would later term her perversity, in obstructing, aborting all his earnest attempts at protection, at maintaining the respectability he believed was indispensable for her as part of the family unit he too belonged to.

Maybe like in her dream, she should have brought Prateek here she thinks, a wicked smile curving across her fragile, delicate features, as she conjures up the scene, picturing Vikram's face as she introduces Prateek to him. Then dismisses the thought. She would need to travel much further from Lalitpur to be able to carry that off. Or maybe ... she has finally come of age, she does not need to make such infantile statements to Vikram. She thinks it as she feels the ghost of the Follower recede into past ... into the indifferent limbo of discarded memories.

YOU CANNOT HAVE ALL THE ANSWERS

"You cannot have all the answers", said the wise woman. "All I can say is, you're going in the wrong direction, foolish one." She was a very wise old woman who had lived long and could even look into the future.

"You may be right, old mother," replied the foolish one. "But ... perhaps I'm not looking for answers – maybe, I want the question to remain a question. To embark on a quest that never attains its goal. For what can be better than striving endlessly? Striving for something which may not be there?"

"You are wasting your life then, foolish one," said the wise woman. "Give up. There are goals which can be fulfilled. Quests that can be ended. Questions answered."

"A question that is answered means the end. A goal fulfilled is death. I want to live, wise mother," the foolish one answered.

"You are the bravest of the brave. Go, I grant you the boon of unrequited love." The wise woman plucked a wilted flower from her hair and gave it to the foolish one, who went forth joyfully.

She would become the moth who singed her wings against the flame. She would become the nightingale sighing for the moon ...

But the wise woman sighed too. Another promising soul lost.

Who was the wise woman? And who was the foolish one? We anticipate perhaps. Because unlike what the old woman said, time answers all questions – or practically all.

Mandira ran down the steps on to the road, twirling the wilted flower in her hand. She wanted to laugh. How amazingly appropriate the gift was! Unrequited love! She was ready to embrace the role of the rejected lover. She would write beautiful poetry, sing sad songs and sigh like a veritable furnace. She saw herself standing at her window, her hair streaming down her back, gazing at the moon. How wonderfully romantic it would be! As romantic as marriage was prosaic. She thought of her parents and pulled a face. How unbearably dull their life together was. *Dal*, *subzi*, *roti* and balancing of accounts. She definitely didn't want to end up like that!

A beggar woman approached her, her face split by a theatrical grimace of woe, whining for a coin. Mandira exclaimed with annoyance. She'd forgotten her purse at home. Laughingly, irreverently, she dumped the flower that was the wise woman's *prasad* into the beggar's tin can. The beggar woman growled, then sucked in her breath in astonishment. The moment the flower touched the can, it clinked. It had turned into a coin, a shining new gold coin. Unable to believe her eyes, she ran after Mandira, who had walked off, striding swiftly as was her wont. She managed to catch up.

A little annoyed, Mandira waved her hands in the air to show that she had nothing else. The beggar woman folded her hands, actually in thanks, but Mandira mistook it to be a plea for more. Glancing around, exasperated, she noticed a young man coming along. He looked like a nice, pleasant fellow. "Excuse me," she said in her forthright way. She was like that, always very direct and straightforward. "Do you have a coin to give this beggar woman?"

The young man was a little taken aback. He had never had a young woman accosting him in the street like that, asking for alms for someone else. But he really was a nice young man and her eager mobile face with its tendrils of hair floating about it moved him so much that he had to give the beggar woman something. He took out a ten rupee note and let it flutter into the tin. The beggar woman was overwhelmed. She fell at Mandira's feet, much to her added annoyance.

"Really, this is too much," she said, shaking her head. "She should be falling at your feet. Thanks awfully, by the way. I forgot my purse at home. Just like me. Terribly absent minded, I am."

The young man beamed. It seemed a delightful quality to him. But Mandira was already turning away. Stop! He wanted to cry out. I have so many things to ask you. But the moment was already slipping by. Their little transaction had come to an end. Then, as luck would have it, he saw something flutter down from her hand. Was it a hankie? What a God sent opportunity! This was classic, absolutely classic. He dived forward. But as he was about to pick it up he realised it was a tissue.

He could have gnashed his teeth. How foolish of him. No one used handkerchiefs any more. What was the protocol with regard to tissues? Would she take offence if he picked it up and gave it to her? Would it be like an accusation of littering? But she must have definitely dropped it by mistake. She didn't look like a litterbug. He was positive she was environmentally aware. This young man, (by the way, his name was Samir) was a committed environmentalist and hated litterbugs. Anyway, since this was the only chance he had of retaining his contact with her, he decided to take the risk.

But no sooner had he scooped up that crumpled little tissue, his eyes almost popped out. Even as he watched, it transformed itself into a beautiful silk scarf. Truly, it was a day for miracles, though little did Mandira, the innocent cause, suspect it!

Samir blinked, shook his head, pinched himself to make sure that he was awake. Then he made a sensible decision. He decided that some kind fairy had decided to take care of his interests and so he ought to proceed in the matter, which he did by running after Mandira and telling her that she'd dropped the silk scarf.

"Oh," she said frowning. "Did I drop this? ... Hmmm – I didn't realise I was wearing this. I must be more absent minded than I realise. Thanks again. It really must be my lucky day, meeting you."

Samir's smile grew even wider. "Please, please," he said quickly before she walked off again. "Can you have a cup of coffee with me?"

Mandira sighed. She really was not in the mood to have cups of coffee with strange young men. But ... actually ... she should have been if she had to avail of her boon of unrequited love. It would give her the opportunity to fall in love with someone who would no doubt spurn her later on. But this was not one of the things she generally did – having cups of coffee with strange young men. In fact she was extraordinarily particular about it. But today was a different sort of a day. She had met the wise woman; she had met the beggar woman and now this young man. Maybe something was meant to come out of this meeting.

Well, as it so happened, something did.

More meetings, to begin with, and many more cups of coffee and lunches and then dinners. But it always puzzled Mandira that Samir would invariably ask her to give him her used up bits of tissue. She thought it some strange quirk in his make up, albeit a harmless one. She also wondered how she happened to drop a scarf that day. She never used them. In fact she didn't possess a single one. Perhaps it was one of those ploys young men used to further acquaintance with young women. She forgave him for that of course. It is always flattering to know that a man is interested enough in you to resort to such tricks. But she couldn't help wondering, did he always roam around with a pretty silk scarf in his pocket in the hope of coming across a girl who caught his fancy? It seemed rather calculating. Also it made him appear a kind of beast always on the prowl. But he had such a charming smile and such long lashed brown eyes that it was easy to forgive him.

Samir on the other hand could never decide if he had witnessed a genuine magical happening or whether he had been hallucinating that day. He became even more confused when she asked him one day with a twinkle in her eye, where he had got the scarf from which he picked up that day.

"From the ground," he said. "You-you dropped it."

"Did I?" she asked and laughed.

A lot of time had passed since that first fateful meeting. Yes, a lot of water had passed under the bridge of their relationship. Now it had reached the stage when she had taken him home to meet her parents and he had taken her home to meet his. Things had gone amicably. No objections had been raised on either side. The two had even begun to look at rings.

But when Mandira laughed in that particular manner, Samir couldn't help feeling stung. In the first place he had never got over his confusion about the tissue changing into the silk scarf. As they had become more intimate he had waited for Mandira to open up and tell him more about it. He had looked out for more magical happenings to occur and when they hadn't, his confusion had grown. Part of Mandira's charm, part of the adventure of knowing her was the prospect that something extraordinary could happen. When it didn't, Samir couldn't help feeling slightly cheated. And yet he continued with the relationship in the hope that some day it might.

So he retaliated by saying, "Don't you know where the scarf came from?"

"How can I?" Mandira shot back. "I never possessed a scarf like that."

"You-you didn't –"

"You know that don't you?"

"I-I don't know."

"Oh stop it! Come clean!"

"What are you trying to say?"

"That you pretended the scarf was mine!" Mandira was nothing if not blunt. "I must say you're quite a character, going around with scarves in your pocket to snare girls."

"Snare girls with scarves in my pocket –" Samir spluttered. "How dare you! You dropped the scarf."

"I don't need to resort to such cheap tricks."

"Yes, you do." In his heart of hearts he knew it was unfair, that she had not dropped the scarf, that she really did not need to resort to such tricks – at least as far as he was concerned. He had felt attracted to her before the scarf incident. But her accusation made him see red.

Well, as often happens with such arguments, they parted in a rage. Because Samir could hardly tell her that a tissue she had dropped had magically turned into a silk scarf. If she wasn't aware of it, wouldn't she have laughed at him if he'd said that?

Broken hearted, Mandira decided to visit the wise woman again. She wanted to confirm that this was what she had meant when she had conferred the boon of unrequited love on her. But when she went to her house, she found the door locked. Sadly she came back on to the street when the same beggar woman, who had haunted the place since then, hoping to find her again, caught sight of her. She rushed forward with her tin can, hoping against hope for the miracle to repeat itself. But today Mandira had not forgotten her purse, so she fumbled inside for some change. Having found some, she was about to drop it into the can, when a ten rupee note slid into it. Astonished, she looked up.

It was Samir. Forlorn, lovesick, he had returned to that place too, since it was the spot that he had first met Mandira.

Mandira looked up. Her eyes met his. And their anger melted away. They returned to the same restaurant for a reconciliatory cup of coffee ...

The day she got married, Mandira thought of the wise woman. What had her words really meant? She thought of her own desire to be the moth singeing her wings against the flame and blushed at her idiocy. Does anyone really want to suffer? And what was so wrong with her parents' life? Everyone had to get married. Unrequited love and such things were pretty themes for poets and story writers. Who wanted to be romantic? One had to live in the real world.

So she began to live in the real world. Where flowers, wilted or otherwise, did not turn into gold coins and discarded tissues into silk scarves. But ... as the days sped past and many questions remained unanswered ... many quests remained unfulfilled and some strange centripetal force made Samir spin further and further away from her, she wondered. Sometimes, she took out the silk scarf from the special box that she had placed it in as a memento of their first wonderful meeting, ran her hand over its soft surface, held it against her cheek and marvelled that something like that could have happened ... once upon a time.

And so their life went on. Having achieved one of the objectives of his life, namely Mandira, Samir went on to accomplish the next – which was success in his career.

And what did Mandira do in the meantime that he pursued his goal with the same single minded persistence that he had pursued Mandira? She lived her life through his, it was enough of a goal for her. She haggled with vegetable vendors and saved his money, brought up his two children with the same commitment that she applied to everything she did, and – she guarded the silk scarf.

Then the day came that she opened the box and found that the scarf had mysteriously transmogrified into a crumpled piece of tissue. Shocked, she turned it over and over in her hand. She was positive, she knew that she had placed it there. Where could it have gone? Who could have taken it and placed a dirty, used tissue in its place? It was not precious or valuable enough for anyone to steal. It was precious only for her. An iron hand clutched her heart, squeezed it mercilessly. Her head spun around, she felt faint. Breathing heavily she laid herself on her bed. Something told her that this boded no good.

Samir came home late that day. He was often late these days.

In fact, lately they'd barely exchanged a few words each day and Mandira had been taking the scarf out more and more to look at it. That's why it gave her such a shock to find it turned into something so unexpected, so bizarre.

She sat up for him that night and in spite of his disinclination for conversation she told him about the missing scarf. He paled when he heard it. Something gripped his heart, too. It was fear, mingled with guilt.

Something had happened. He knew what it was, in fact he could perhaps state the exact minute when the silk scarf went back to being the ordinary disposable object it originally was. He had been in bed with another woman at the time. But what could he tell Mandira? She would not believe him if he decided to tell her the story of the silk scarf now. And he certainly could not tell her why it had changed back.

The magical happening that he had been waiting for had occurred, but not in the way he would have liked it to.

"Are you sure you didn't keep it anywhere else?" he asked, falsely and glibly. Unfortunately, he had lived too and come a long way from being the warm hearted young man Mandira had first encountered. "Check your cupboard thoroughly tomorrow."

"I've checked it!" Mandira wailed.

"Check it again," he said, turning his back. "Mandira, I'm very tired, very sleepy." He shrank away from her and lay sleepless for a long time. What, who was Mandira? If only he could part company from her. He couldn't stand the thought of these peculiar happenings. In any case the other woman attracted him much more now. But – but would, could Mandira take some kind of revenge? If not she, the magic that imbued their relationship might turn on him in some way. The thought chilled him and eventually prevented him from abandoning Mandira physically, though he had already cast her aside in his heart.

Mandira knew something momentous happened that day when the silk scarf vanished never to return. The silken bond which had tied them together ... Samir turned more and more cold and distant. Their lives grew further and further apart. Was the wise woman's boon granted at last ... when she did not want it any more? Too late she learned the lesson, that one shouldn't speak without thinking. But oh, the brashness of lion-hearted youth, the prudence of old age shrivels up before its heat. One gains wisdom when it'd too late to put it to any use.

The wise woman is too old now. She's senile, in fact. Mandira knows it's no use going to her. But she couldn't help thinking of what she had said ... "You can never have all the answers ... " True, Samir could not supply her with the answer to the riddle of the silk scarf. Yet she had understood what it meant. That something precious had turned into dross. And hadn't she said she did not want any answers? That a question answered was like death? Was this, then the end of it all?

The thought left her numb, as still and silent, inside and out, as a stone. It seemed horrifyingly strange that she should have known that day of her ignorant, restless youth, known what lay ahead of her. That she should have received what she had asked for.

Then she thought of the wilted flower that the wise woman had given her, the symbol of blighted love. How thoughtlessly she had dropped it into the beggar woman's tin can. But ... the woman had been so grateful ... so grateful ...

Something drew her out of the house towards the spot where she had met the beggar woman and then Samir. It seemed a futile quest. The beggar woman would not be there after all those years. The place itself would have changed. And the wise woman had moved away. Yet she went.

She went and stood there and looked around. Yes, the place had changed. It looked more crowded, more prosperous, but dirtier. But ... the beggar woman was nowhere to be seen ... Mandira waited, waited for a long time. She was turning away dispiritedly when a woman came running from somewhere and said, "You, is it really you?"

She fell at Mandira's feet. Mandira was flabbergasted. Why was this dignified grey-haired woman doing that? Was she crazy? Of course she had no way of knowing that it was the beggar woman who was no longer the beggar woman. She had a fruit stall now. "Thanks to you," she said.

"But how?" Mandira asked, puzzled.

"You remember the gold coin," she looked around and lowered her voice now, "the wilted flower that you changed into a gold coin with your wonderful power?"

"The wilted flower that changed into a gold coin!" Mandira felt her hair stand on end. Had she really accomplished that? No wonder the beggar woman had been so grateful!

"I held on to it for some time," the beggar woman continued. "Since it was a magical thing. Then one day it occurred to me that even if it was magical, you must have given for some purpose. Maybe you wanted me to stop begging. I sold it and started selling fruit. Little by little my business grew. Now I own twenty fruit stalls. But I always man this one personally. I have always lived in the hope that one day you will return ... "

Mandira sighed. Strange were the ways of fortune. But some things had to be clarified, credit given where it was due. "I gave you a wilted flower," she said. "It was the wise woman's magic that turned it into a golden coin. Or maybe it was fate. For me it was meant to be a wilted flower, for you a golden coin."

"Whatever it was, I received it from your hands, hence all my gratitude goes out to you," the woman persisted.

She insisted on packing a huge basket of fruit for Mandira.

Mandira went home, marvelling at the ways of fortune. As she sat in her big empty house staring at the basket of fruit, suddenly something came to her. If the beggar woman could strive and multiply a gold coin into twenty fruit stalls surely she could manage some arithmetic of her own? Or was she perpetually doomed to possess useless objects like wilted flowers and crumpled tissues? On the other hand, though, hadn't she asked for them? Why oh why, hadn't she listened to the wise woman?

However ... it was too late for regrets. So she lived on, in spite of Samir, in spite of the loss of the silk scarf.

But ... little did she guess why she could live on ... guess that the foolish one had changed ... she had acquired knowledge ... in fact, she had become a wise woman herself. She had learnt that if you don't want answers you will not get any ... and that ... actually you don't need any. Because ... life is for living ... not just loving ...

THE ABORTION

The doctor's waiting room was painted a pistachio green. Perhaps it was meant to be soothing. But I found it nauseating, like the pictures of the impossibly pink and bonny babies that decorated the walls. They didn't look human to me – someone's grotesque idea of the perfect infant – as remote from reality as a celluloid doll is from a real, live, breathing baby.

Snatching up a two month-old magazine, I tried to concentrate on it, just to shut out my surroundings. But try as I did, I could not shut out the nasal tones of the ghazal singer, wailing insistently at me via a strategically placed speaker, or the murmuring of the other inmates' voices.

Cool, crisp cotton saris, languid chiffons, smoothly flowing salwar kameezes – covering all manner and size of pregnancies. Large, small, medium, gently rounded, aggressively protuberant, painfully prominent. I'd never thought the sight of pregnant women in the plural could be so terrifying.

An ominous warning kept flashing through my mind, as irritatingly insistent as neon sign. This could be – this would be – me, if I failed to act in time. The worst was, they looked so smug and secure, accompanied by proprietary looking mothers-in-law or proud, smirking husbands. The little fathers-to-be. So pleased with themselves. Curious glances flickered at me: I was so obviously alone.

A feeling of overpowering suffocation came over me. I wanted to get up and run. But where to? There was no way I could escape my problem. Besides I'd been running from it long enough. As though by ignoring the damn thing, it would just vanish on its own. Could one wish an unwanted pregnancy away? Goodness knows I'd tried.

In fact, if I hadn't fainted that day on my way to the bus-stop, I probably wouldn't have been here – in the pistachio green room – sweating profusely in spite of the air conditioning. I would still have trying some mumbo-jumbo to solve my problem. Like wearing pure white saris as though some perverse force would not be able to resist staining them with menstrual blood and bring me deliverance. Or forcing food down my unwilling throat as if the nausea wasn't there forcing it out again.. A kind of desperate magic that wouldn't work.

Then the silly home remedies I'd heard about, running up and down the stairs, carrying heavy weights, hot and cold baths – they'd all proved useless.

It was the fainting incident that did it. Forced the painful certainty of it all on me. Finding myself flat on the ground suddenly, when just a moment before I had been chatting with Sumi, my friend. The ground felt scratchy and hard beneath my face. I could taste mud and blood from my cut lip. And as people helped me to my feet, a scene from an old Hindi movie flashed through my mind. The hapless heroine becoming aware of her condition in a similar manner. But I'd known all along, hadn't I?

"What happened?" Sumi asked, shocked and bewildered, as she helped me into a three wheeler, a worried frown creasing her broad forehead.

I didn't want to talk. My head ached. The taste of blood was sickeningly strong in my mouth. I knew I'd have to act soon, before it was too late ...

"Parul!" The loud voice jerked me back to the present. It was the receptionist beckoning with a synthetic smile. Somehow I managed to totter along on suddenly rubbery legs, to face first a barrage of questions, then a battery of tests. And eventually I found myself spread on the examination table, legs ignonimously drawn up, trying not to flinch from the probing fingers.

"H'mm," the doctor said. She was rather smartly got up, smelt almost overpoweringly of perfume and had a carefully cultivated manner. Guessing this was the signal for me to get up, I clambered off and tried to rearrange my clothing and my dignity. Heart-in- mouth, I approached her desk. You see, I hadn't given up hope completely. Maybe she'd say it was all a silly mistake...

She beamed at me from behind her trendy specs. "You're

definitely pregnant," she said happily. "The tests will confirm it, I'm sure."

I tried to stretch my congealing lips into an answering smile. I could see her opening and closing her mouth – but could not hear the words. All my senses were numbed. Little did she know that what she thought were tidings of joy, were actually a knock-out blow. Then I realised that she was staring at me strangely. So I quickly nodded and grabbed the paper she was holding out. Handing over what seemed like an exorbitant fee, I fled the place.

The humid heat outside made me gasp. But I walked on blindly for quite a while till a wave of nausea made me stop short. I had to get home. But it was only when I was rattling home in the three wheeler that I realised that I had forgotten to arrange for the abortion!

"You dummy!" Sumi said, when I got home. We shared not only the barsati flat but also our deepest confidences. "You should have gone to one of those clinics – you know those –"

With uncharacteristic delicacy she left out the word 'abortion'. I was grateful. The word itself conjured up all sorts of horrors. Grim faced females preparing to attack one with knitting needles, shifty eyed quacks operating in foul smelling rooms – the stuff of all the gloomy fiction on the subject one had read. I pictured myself bleeding to death in some back alley and shivered. Even though I knew it needn't be that way. I forced myself to recall what one of my married colleagues had once said. "It's no big deal ... I went and had an ice cream as soon as I came out. It's perfectly safe and painless ..."

But somehow I hated the thought of going to one of those places. It seemed so horribly obvious. "What are you going to do now?" Sumi demanded. "And – aren't you going to tell him?"

"No!" The answer jerked out spontaneously. True, he had helped to create this problem. But an odd revulsion had been growing in me ever since I suspected what was wrong with me. Somewhat perversely, when I could have done with his help I wanted nothing whatsoever to do with him. I could not understand it myself, but the feeling was so strong, so overpowering, that I could not fight it even if I wanted to. I'd have to deal with it myself, all on my own.

"I'll find another doctor," I said, meeting Sumi's anxious, puzzled gaze. I couldn't face the thought of meeting those pasted on smiles again. I'd noticed another gynaecologist's signboard on my way to work. That's where I headed.

Experience made me confident, but the place made me uneasy. Shabby, down- at- heel, there were no fancy trimmings here, no chummy first name familiarity. The clientele was a little mixed, unlike the uniform prosperity the other place had displayed. The seats were covering with cheap rexine, gashed in some places and the walls grimy with the oil from the countless heads which had leaned against it.

But somehow the doctor restored my confidence. A tired looking woman with grey hair escaping from a bun, her movements were brisk and efficient.

Again, I went through the routine. But before she could

pronounce the verdict, I blurted out, "I want an abortion."

She stared at me for a moment. "Are you quite sure?"

"Absolutely," I replied, holding her gaze. "As soon as possible."

"All right," she nodded, asking no further questions, as though she had guessed my predicament. "Thursday, 8.30 a.m.," she said consulting a diary. "Come with an empty stomach."

The relief felt unreal. I couldn't wait to tell Sumi about it.

"I-I'll come with you," she said.

"Thanks." I was really grateful. Because a sudden unease was fluttering up, chilling the edges of my being. I didn't want it to progress further, turn me into a block of fearful ice.

Thursday. Did it arrive soon or did the wait stretch out painfully? I'm not sure. It seemed too long to wait for deliverance, to be free of this thing growing inexorably inside me. To be free of those nightmarish fears, saved from disastrous consequences. But the dread that wanted me to put off the moment forever. It would insist on creeping up on me and obiliterate the feelings of anticipated relief.

I woke up bright and early that day. We reached the nursing home well before time. The place – sparklingly clean, in contrast to the clinic – was just coming alive. Floors being swabbed, nurses bustled about importantly, breakfast trays rattled their ways into rooms.

As we waited, tense, the high wail of a new-born infant pierced through the silence. A curious flutter rose from my stomach up to my throat. Goose pimples blistered my skin, for a moment I thought I'd choke. It had never occurred to me that this thing inside me could grow into something like that baby ...

But the doctor appeared just then, distracting me from that uncomfortable trend of thought. Still in her dressing gown, she looked worn out, as though she'd been up all night.

She nodded to me. "Be with you in moment," she said. Then a nurse came along, "Come with me," she said.

Irrationally, I wanted to escape. All the horror stories surfaced again ... what were they going to do to me? A last frightened look at Sumi and I was hustled away.

Wearing their gown I was led into a room with a terrifying array of instruments. A needle pricked my arm, then a blessed blackness descended ...

I came to life to find an anxious Sumi bending over me.

"Is it – is it done?" I asked uncertainly.

She nodded.

"I'm fine," I said, producing an extra large smile for her benefit.

But it was only after I'd paid and left the place that elation really swept over me. It's over, I thought, light headed with relief. I've been saved. How simple it seemed now, almost an anti-climax! What happened to the gory stuff? I almost felt cheated .

Even the city looked transformed as we drove home in a cab. A shower of rain had washed the dust off the trees and the bushes and everything looked fresh and green and new – like me.

A dull pain was beginning to throb inside. I welcomed it. It was proof of my newly cleansed self. And then, I had pain killers if it went out of hand. But it was only when I lay in bed as I'd been told to – that the sound began to ring in my ears. The cry of an infant, a thin, high pitched wailing.

"Sumi," I asked, "Where's that baby crying?"

She gave me a peculiar look. "There's no baby crying," she said.

I put the pillows over my head but I couldn't shut it out. She's wrong, I thought. There is a baby crying. Because the sound came back, again and again and again – grating on my senses.

Then I realised what that cry was. It was the baby that hadn't been born, that I hadn't – that I couldn't allow to be born. What had it been – girl or boy? Thin, chubby, pretty, playful, naughty ...? I'd never know, would I? Never, ever ...

The sudden wetness of tears trickling down my cheeks jolted me back to my senses. I sat up ... the sound began to fade. You stupid, stupid fool, I thought. It never existed, it never was real ... it was a menace ...

I repeated it over and over again like a mantra, and finally it worked. The sound faded out as I lay down and drifted into a deep, dreamless sleep ...

IF THE EARTH SHOULD MOVE ...

She had never learned to swim. But she dreamt, often, of floating on a wide expanse of water – formless fluid holding her up – she moving along with its motion – the sun on her face – dancing on the water – a million restless specks of fragmented light ...

The earth, solid, firm, hard, held you upright and still. You could sit or lie down upon it, inhaling the scent of grass and soil, or roll on it, but the motion would be yours. The earth seldom moves. And when it does, it's disaster.

And what about the air? The air cannot hold you up. You cannot fly like a bird. But there are times when it presses against you, stopping your breath, thick as the earth. Encases you like a prison wall – the air you breathe, the air that is your life. It moves, of course, but does not carry you along like water – the primeval fluid in which we were all formed and lived ...

Mansi felt the baby move with terrific force, tear its way out of her, forcing an enormous scream from her throat. A cry she could not arrest, even if she tried. It went on and on, like a stone, suddenly dislodged, tumbling down a hill, which cannot stop till it reaches the bottom. Only when there was no more sound left within her to wrench out, did it stop.

Then she became conscious of another sound – the baby's long thin wail. It made her feel strangely light headed. Another being entering the world. Suddenly she felt a great weariness, as if she already knew what lay ahead of her and sure enough, the very next minute the doctor spoke. "You've had another girl," she said.

The air crushed Mansi down with its weight ...

That night she dreamt that she was swimming. She was swimming in a lake surrounded by tall hills. It was a sunny day. The sky was a transparent blinding blue and ahead of her a man moved along, rowing a boat. He wore a short sleeved T-shirt and she could see that his arms were thickly muscled. So was his smoothly moving back. The boat cut through the water effortlessly, leaving a frothy wake. She badly wanted to see the man's face. In fact she was following the boat just because she was so eager to see what he looked like ... if the face fulfilled the promise of that body ...

The baby was pretty. All her daughters were pretty, luckily or unluckily. For a woman, beauty was both a blessing and a curse. She thought of the matrimonial columns in the newspapers, all repetitions of "... wanted tall, fair, beautiful girl ... " There was something so vapidly monotonous about it.

One day, she was sure, some high-tech whiz kid would set up a factory to clone the perfect female to satisfy this hunger for tall, fair, beautiful girls.

Her cousin Nisha could have been the perfect model for one of those cloning factories. Nisha who had introduced her to the glitzy glamour of stars' lives via the film magazines. She hadn't realised at the time that Nisha had had aspirations herself. That she was deeply conscious of her own beauty, of the fact that she was star material. That she felt she only needed a hand up from the right quarter, which had not been forthcoming so far. In the tiny *mofussil* town where they lived, what opportunity was there for a girl to further such ambitions?

Nisha had been staying with them at the time. At eleven, Mansi hadn't really been aware of the fact that there had been a particular reason behind Nisha's frequent visits. She had got used to her staying with them more than with her own family.

Till the day ... she got a hint ... when she overheard her talking to her mother. She had sounded frantic, "*Mausi*, please, please don't send me back!"

The urgency in her voice had sent something crawling up Mansi's back, made her stomach crumple into a tiny, painful ball. A horrible sensation that told her with plummeting certainty that things were not quite what they seemed. That something ugly and unknown lay beneath the seemingly natural sequence of Nisha's stays. The playful camaraderie that she shared with her, despite the fact that she was almost eight years her senior, which had been growing into a closer, tighter bond during those unscheduled, unexpected visits, suddenly seemed false and unreal, because Nisha had never told her ...

"But your mother wants you back," Ma had sounded equally frantic. "How can I refuse her?"

"I am eighteen now," that stubborn note had come into Nisha's voice. Mansi knew that note. It meant that nothing could move her now. "I can do what I want. Get married if I wish to. No one can stop me."

"Do what you want," her mother's voice had turned hard. "But do it at your parents' place."

"Parents? Parents' place?" Nisha's voice had sounded mocking. She had laughed harshly. A sound like the dry rasp of fallen leaves, suddenly disturbed by an unexpected breeze.

Mansi had felt an unexpected anger burgeon up, against her mother. Why was she forcing Nisha didi to go back when she didn't want to?

One thing she could guess at, quite easily, why Nisha wouldn't want to go back. Because she had a stepfather. Stepfathers were almost unheard of, in the world in which they lived, it was very unusual having one. But Mansi could well believe that they could be as cruel as the proverbial stepmother.

"Nisha didi," she had whispered that night as they snuggled together in bed. "Does he beat you?

"Beat me – who?"

"Your – um ... *Mausa* ... "

"Beat me – no, he wouldn't dare – the creep – " She had let out a long jagged sigh, piercing as a shard of broken glass. "I hate him, I hate him, I hate him – " she'd stopped abruptly.

"Doesn't *Mausi* tell him not to be mean to you?"

A short bitter laugh. "*Mausi*! *Mausi* can't tell anybody anything. And – she's not going to tell me either!"

All the same Nisha, had had to go. She had looked grim when she left, her eyes had stared blankly through Mansi when she said good bye, as if she weren't there at all. Mansi'd felt hurt. Wasn't Nisha didi sorry to leave her?

A neighbour had happened to be travelling that way. She'd been put in his charge. After all, a young girl could hardly be permitted to travel alone.

It had turned out to be a disastrous choice. Some time later the news came that the two had eloped. The neighbour had abandoned his wife for Nisha. Ma said she would never be able to hold up her head again. She publicly declared that she had broken off all connection with Nisha. Her name was never mentioned again in the house and Mansi had never dared to ask ...

And then, years and years later, by some bizarre twist of fate, she had found her again. Married now, Mansi was living in Bombay, a place as remote, as far removed as it was possible, from the small town in which she had grown up. The mother of two girls herself, she had recognised the plumpish matron with a teenaged daughter in tow when she glimpsed her by chance in a store. Because Nisha's amazing beauty was still more or less intact. Respectably married now, to a man much older than her. Mansi had never been able to discover exactly what he did for a living, though. Nisha had been evasive.

Mansi swam and swam but could not catch up with the man. She was not able to see his face ...

Saurabh hid his disappointment well. He picked up the baby and stroked her soft cheek, "She looks like you," he said. Mansi tried to smile, despite the sense of failure that weighed her down.

Was he the man in the dream, who would not show his face, she wondered? In a sense, it would be like him. He was good at concealing his essential self. In all these years of living together, she hadn't found out what he was really like. But, no, he did not have such a spectacular body. Was she secretly hankering for another man? What was it like sleeping with two different men? Nisha would know ...

Ultimately, the neighbour had gone back to his wife. But Ma had never spoken to him again. She held him responsible for 'spoiling' Nisha.

"A married man! We trusted him to look after her like a sister," Mansi had heard her telling her friend Mrs. Sharma. "Imagine my position. Nisha's mother stopped talking to me – my one and only sister. That just shows no man can be trusted."

But was Nisha totally blameless? Mansi had wondered. Of course, you could blame it on her pretty face. But even Mansi had noticed the coy glances she threw at Ravi bhaiya, another neighbour's son. But would she have deliberately thrown herself at a married man? That was what had always troubled Mansi.

Of course, later, much later when certain facts had become clear to her, she had not wondered at her desperation.

"We were sleeping outside. It was summer. I felt someone fumbling at the string of my *salwar*. I was about to scream, when he pressed my mouth shut. I thrashed about hard enough to almost topple the bed over. But you know Ma ... she sleeps like a log ..."

Perhaps Nisha had thought the neighbour a better option if she had to put up with someone ...

"She's a darling, really sweet, mmmm," Nisha kissed the baby noisily. For some reason Saurabh didn't really like her visiting Mansi, but could hardly stop her. "She'll grow up to be a beauty, a star."

Mansi had not been able to hold back a sigh. "Why are you sighing?" Nisha had demanded. "Thank God for this lovely baby."

Lovely baby, lovely baby. Sometimes she was the swimmer and sometimes the lake. The baby swam out of her thrashing wildly. The man in the boat paddled on and on ...

"Do you know I went to see him when he was sick, dying?" Nisha said. "I-I did get in touch with Ma after some time ... a long, long time, actually ... after all ... she was my mother." There was a strange, inscrutable look on her face. "Ma insisted that I come. She said he was very eager to see me. He caught hold of my hand. I almost threw up. 'Forgive me' he said. Ma told me 'He cared for you like his own daughter and you stabbed him in the back like that. We would have got you married in the best way possible. Found you a proper man. You cut off all our noses. We had no face left to show anyone.' I didn't know whether to laugh or to cry. Only ... only Sonu, my brother understood. 'I know why you went, Nisha didi,' he said. He wept. 'If I'd been a little older ... but I was too scared of him.' Did you know he used to 'discipline' Sonu?" Nisha went on. "Everyone used to praise him ... said he was saint, taking on a widow with two children and not having any of his own. All bullshit. There was something wrong with him I think. He couldn't have any, I think ... That's why he felt so safe ... with me ... "

Sometimes, when Saurabh lay next to her, holding her close, she felt a smooth syrupy contentment steal over her. The same sensation she had when she swam through her dreams. The sun seeping through her limbs, floating along with the diamond studded current, further and further ...

But that night, the unexpected happened. She felt herself tiring as she swam. She heard someone crying ... was it herself? Or was it the baby? She could feel it burrowing into her breast. The soft little rosebud mouth turned surprisingly hard when it latched on to her nipples. It tugged and tugged, frantic to get as much as it could out of her ...

No, life is not a straightforward motion, a river flowing onwards. It's a zigzagging movement back and forth – leaving the past to embrace the future but coming face to face with it again just when you begin to believe you've rounded the bend.

Nisha'd made a clean start but yet, the past hung around her like an odour, a whiff of something stale, which keeps surfacing no matter how much you try to scrub it away.

"I sometimes wonder why I went off with Naresh. But at the time he seemed the only option left to me. It was him or back to that ... he swore he was crazy about me. I believed him. *Mausi* must have been furious."

Her large, questioning eyes were shadowed with an ancient pain.

Mansi nodded expressionlessly, not meeting her gaze. She felt an unexpected guilt stab her, as though she had been a part of that anger, that ostracisation. She reached out to stroke the baby's arm feeling its soft little hand closing tightly around her finger. How strong that instinct was ... to hold on, to clutch for support. Had Nisha felt like that at the time ... ? Had she clung on to Naresh like a drowning man clutches at the proverbial straw?

"He said he'd take me to Bombay. He had an uncle in the film line. He would help me, he said, give me a break. He said, 'You're more beautiful than any film star ... ' Nisha's eyes seemed to float off, far away, as if she were re-entering that distant time. The moment swung between them, like an indolent pendulum, then slowly carried them back to the present. Nisha shook her head hard, blinked, sniffed surreptitiously. Mansi could feel her heart, a cold lump of iron pressing against her chest ... "We came here, to Bombay ..." her voice sounded hollow and distant, as if it were coming out of the past ... "But the uncle had moved. We could not find his new address ... "

Nisha stopped there. As if those things that remained, were best left unsaid, even now, at a time so far removed that they almost seemed unreal. Mansi tried to imagine what had happened, how they had coped. And what had ultimately made Naresh abandon Nisha to return to his young wife and child and of course, his parents. He had a safe niche waiting for him in his father's business. And then, everything is forgiven the prodigal son ... he is always welcomed back.

But the prodigal daughter ... Can she find her way home? No. For her coming back is much more complicated. In any case, Nisha, the perennial wanderer, had never had a home in that sense. So she had stayed back, battling the tide that threatened to sweep her away into some anonymous whirlpool of annihilation, the best way she could. She never spoke about that time, not even how she met her husband ... But something made Mansi feel, that whatever it was, that marriage was in a sense an act of desperation too, the way the elopement with Naresh was. With the difference that while that was an attempt to move on, this was an effort to find permanence, root herself to the earth ...

She was reaching the other shore. The boat was just a little ahead of her now. She felt a pleasurable anticipation. At last the man would show his face. ·Maybe she would be able to talk to him ... The boat slid on ... went to rest with a jerk against the shore. Mansi put in the last spurt of effort. The man drew the oars in, rose up in the boat. He turned around ... but ... just then, the baby cried,waking her up ...

The man is walking somewhere in the mountains. He paces through the woods with a swinging, easy stride. The road leads upwards, higher and higher. Mansi has left the lovely, fluid, formless lake behind and is toiling up after the man. On the firm, too solid earth ...

The baby is sound asleep now, but she can feel Saurabh pressing into her, making the man fade. Stop, stop, she wants to say. I want to see his face. But he presses deeper and deeper, clutches her milk swollen breasts ...

Mansi gives up. She'll never see the man's face ... Maybe ... she doesn't want to any more ... Did Nisha see any of their faces, examine them carefully? Perhaps she didn't want to either. But ... if she had looked harder she might have found what lay behind them ... and maybe something did, beyond what was obvious, in one of theirs' at least ... And if she had, perhaps the earth might have moved and carried her along in formless, fluid motion like the water, to some extraordinary, unknown plane of experience which transcended the present ... to something better perhaps ... who knew? But what was better – had she herself found out – in the course of her own mundane, boringly blameless, totally unspotted existence? That constant swimming through the even current of her life, searching for the man who would not show his face. Never ... ever ... would the earth move for her either. But did she really want it to? She had yet to find out. Because she really didn't know what she would do if the earth should actually move.

It could be disaster ...

THE STUFF OF DREAMS

"Why do you think we have dreams? Do they mean anything as people say?" asked the young woman whose name was Ketaki.

"Dreams are given to us to save our lives, ' the old woman replied. She seemed lost in a dream herself when she said this.

'But what if a dream remains incomplete? Or if it's a bad dream? How can a nightmare save our lives?" asked the young woman scornfully. She studied the old woman's face with an impatient frown. "I'm talking about real dreams, the type you have when you're asleep."

The old woman's face was scored and crisscrossed with so many lines that one could get lost tracing their course. Trying to find where one ended and the other began would be like trying to find a way out of the maze of time itself. Ketaki had tried – often enough but been compelled to give up each time.

"No dream is ever false," said the old woman after a long

time. "The dreamer may be false to the dream but not the dream to the dreamer. Because – the dream is you, the essential, inner you ..."

Ketaki sat up suddenly, jerking her hair out of the old woman's hands. She was oiling her hair. Ketaki had long and lustrous hair and the old woman got much pleasure out of handling it. As a professional masseuse, her services were not as much in demand any more as they used to be and as it was she hardly ever got the opportunity to play with such long hair.

"'I had a dream last night," Ketaki said irritably. "I don't think it was given to me to save my life." She was disappointed in the old woman. She was simply looking for comfort but the old woman nattered too much, gave too much unsought for advice. She made such a big deal of her wisdom and experience but came up with so many nonsensical-sounding statements that Ketaki was inclined to believe that she was growing senile. She certainly was old enough. ""I believe," she continued, "It was given to me to frighten me out of my wits, not save my life. That I could do such a mad thing-even in a dream! The thought! As if I was not afraid enough." She shuddered. ""If only I knew what it meant. You know so many people, do you know anyone who interprets dreams?"

"Ah, so that's what you want ..." the old woman said. 'Well, a dream may be a portent, it may be a riddle, but are you sure you want to know? It may not be what you want to hear ..." she added in a softer voice.

'Of course I do! Why else do you think I'm asking you?"

Ketaki said, ignoring the last sentence.

"Sometimes it' s better not to know too much," the old woman went on, her voice dry. "But tell me your dream."

She massaged Ketaki's head in a smooth, circular motion. The young woman felt a languorous peace steal over her. The old woman might talk too much but she was good at her work. Ketaki's head hurt. She'd been up half the night attending to her husband's needs, which were many. They left her with very little time to sleep, to recoup from the stressful events of the day.

She'd massaged his legs. Then she had suckled him at her breast like a babe. When she was done with that he wanted to crawl into the dark soft place she had which made him forget all his troubles. Sometimes it seemed that he wanted to stay there forever. But he was her husband so she had to do all this for him. She wasn't sure if the headache was the result of to little sleep or the unfinished dream. An unfinished dream leaves you with a sense of frustration, a feeling of incompleteness, a yearning almost as unbearable as unfinished loving.

"Tell me the dream,' the old woman said. "'I know a little about dreams and what they mean."

"I dreamt that I was walking in the marketplace and a madwoman came up to me. Her hair was knotted and wild, her face caked with dirt, flies buzzed about her in swarms. She wore a dirty old blanket wrapped around herself, a thick grey blanket," Ketaki spoke rapidly as if she wanted to finish telling it as fast as she could. "But when I looked into her red rimmed eyes which were so large and untamed, I froze. Something in her eyes held me – as if it was something I could recognise, identify with. Strange, isn't it – what would I have in common with a madwoman from the streets?"

She seemed to address the question to herself but the old woman, the garrulous old woman had to answer. "Yes," she said, sounding more like an echo than a person answering a question. "What would you have in common with a madwoman of the streets?" Her voice was blank, as empty and expressionless as an echo.

"And as I stood there watching her she made a sudden movement and the blanket fell open." Ketaki paused,as if to reconsider what she was saying. Her voice quivered as she finally said, "With a shock I realised that she wore nothing underneath that blanket – nothing at all!"

"'Nothing at all," repeated the old woman. Oddly enough she didn't sound at all surprised. She knew more about the ways of madwomen than the young woman who had always lived immured within the safe walls of her house. Unlike the old woman whose work took her here and there, through the busy streets, in and out of houses. She knew practically all there was to know from the business of the streets to the secrets in the big, safe houses, which swarmed as much with secrets as the sewers with cockroaches. Secrets which belied their promise of safety.

The young woman sucked in her breath. "I don't know what I felt at that moment," she said, "looking at her nakedness, thinking of her roaming the streets with nothing more than a blanket between her and the world. But whatever I felt at that moment was very strong – so I reached out and took hold of her hand and led her home ... I thought I'd give her some clothes to wear, you see ... clothes which would give her some kind of protection. A woman without clothes is so exposed!"

"How kind, what a kind little woman," murmured the old one. She rubbed Ketaki's head hard, so hard that it shook. But the young woman didn't seem to notice and went on, narrating the story of her dream.

'Well, I took her straight into the bathroom, and pulled off her dirty old blanket and flung it out of the window. I can't tell you how good I felt when I threw the filthy thing away. At that moment I could imagine what the madwoman would feel like when she was nice and clean dressed in fresh, new clothes – if a madwoman can understand what that feels like! But it would make me feel much better to see her decently dressed. The thought of another woman so exposed is scary. What had really upset me was the fact that she didn't seem to mind at all, roaming the streets like that all naked under the blanket. She didn't say anything at all when I took her by the hand and led her home. She just clutched my hand as tightly as she could and came along, as trusting as a child. In fact, I had to pry her fingers off when I put her under the shower ... I hope you understand what I'm saying," she said turning around to look into the old woman's face. "In this dream I took this dirty, filthy madwoman into my own beautiful bathroom with its gold and white tiles and stood her under my own shower!"

"'I understand," the old woman nodded. "'I understand very

well." There was a touch of asperity in her voice. "I also understand that it was a dream."

'Of course it was a dream! Didn't I tell you right in the beginning? But I can't tell you how vivid this dream is still in my mind. It feels as if it really happened." She shivered a little. 'Now –" The young woman paused, she ran her pointed red tongue over lips as if they felt dry suddenly. "She didn't seem to know what to do, you understand? She was that mad. She didn't even know that she had to wash herself. So I had to do it for her. I had to pick up the soap and rub it over her body, scrub her clean. I felt a little odd, but I had to do it. I had committed myself to making her clean and fresh again. But ... " The young woman paused again, "My clothes get wet, so I took them off. I thought, what the hell, we were just two woman together and she was mad in any case."

"What logic – such logic in a dream," the old woman murmured.

"Why can't there be logic in dreams?" the young woman demanded, a little miffed. "I'm a logical person, you know, and also a kind person, even though I say so myself. Who would want to handle a dirty, mad woman? It's risky, you know handling a mad person. Who knows when they might turn around and attack you? I'm brave too, you know," she added as if just discovering that about herself. "And in any case-don't I take off my clothes for you to massage me?"

"Yes you do, yes you do," the old woman' s head seemed to wag on its own. "And yes, my dear, you are kind and brave, very kind and brave." She stroked the young woman's soft cheek gently. Her hand felt rather rough and scratchy for a masseuse. "'But I hope you're not forgetting that it was a dream."

"Certainly not!" The young woman sounded injured. "Do you think I would do such things in real life?"

"No you wouldn't," the old woman sounded sad. "I doubt it, very much."

"By the way –"the young woman said softly. "She had a beautiful body. Can you imagine," she said wonderingly, "A madwoman with a beautiful body. Such high, full breasts, such a slim waist ..."

"Why not?" replied the old woman softly. So softly that the young woman did not hear what she said after that. "Why can't or why shouldn't a madwoman have a beautiful body?" A little louder, she said, "Take off your blouse my dear, so I can massage your back now."

The young woman complied, dutifully. She had a beautiful body too, even though she was not mad. "Ah-h ..." she said, as the old woman rubbed her back. "That feels so-o good!" The old woman's hands felt softer now ... going up and down, up and down her back ... soothing all the pain away.

"Well –" the young woman continued, "After I had finished soaping her – mind you – it was like bathing a small child who is unable to bathe herself." She giggled a little hysterically. "'A small child with breasts and – and pubic hair." Then she stopped laughing and became a little serious. Actually more than a little serious. She looked quite grim as a matter of fact. "While I was trying to bathe her I couldn't help noticing that there was blood congealed between her legs ... She'd been – had –"

"We've all been had!" the old woman cried out, so shrill and sudden that the young woman started and let out a little shriek herself. "And we all bleed when we're had, outwardly or inwardly. I've been had so many times that I've lost count! And I've bled so much –"

"Oh shut up, who wants to keep count of all that," the young woman replied brusquely. "I certainly don't. I'd rather forget such things. And if I can return to my dream please, we're not talking about your bleeding but the madwoman's."

"Of course, you can," the old woman sounded annoyed. Maybe there was something more she wanted to say but the young woman was not letting her. And that can be as frustrating for a garrulous old woman as an unfinished dream or incomplete loving for a young one – because after all, ultimately what else is left but words?

"I felt more than a little sick, you know, seeing that. But I had to finish the job. I'd begun to clean her up and I would complete my job as best I could, especially since the poor thing was no more competent than a child. She whimpered and squirmed a little at first, then she seemed to like it – being cleaned up, you know. Then suddenly she began to think that she should do the same thing to me – Imagine!" The young woman's laugh rang out, sharp and clear. "Wasn't it weird? The poor child ..."

"Weird indeed," said the old woman a little absent mindedly, as if she were preoccupied with all she couldn't say, all that was going round and round in her mind, the undigested thoughts she couldn't spew out as words, tumbling about here and there inside her head. "You get yourself massaged every day," she suddenly said, "And your body will remain young and alive forever."

"'Too bad you couldn't do the same for yourself," the young woman said unkindly. She was furious that the old woman would insist on interpolating her stray thoughts into her narrative, disturbing the flow. She also sensed an ulterior motive, a pecuniary one, and she didn't like being reminded of the fact that one day *she* might be like the old woman criss-crossed with wrinkles.

"'Who knows what I could or couldn't do for myself?" the old woman replied indifferently. "But you haven't told me the rest of your dream."

"What is there to tell? Just another senseless dream." The young woman sounded quite irritable. Then she softened. She did want to tell someone and the old woman was the only one she could talk to. "Well, I told you what she was doing to me," she giggled. 'And then what do you think happened?"

"What?"

"My husband came home and caught us."

'What!"

"I'd forgotten to bolt the door, imagine. Wasn't it silly of me? He was angry, so angry, I can't tell you –"

"He was? In your dream?"

"Then –" Ketaki went on as if she hadn't heard. "After I'd flung on some clothes – I told him the whole story – how I'd felt sorry for the madwoman and brought her home to clean her up, he understood. I think he understood. At least I hope so. But – he said I couldn't keep her. You know ... I'd thought I could keep her, felt it was my duty to keep her, she wasn't safe on the streets ... she needed someone to take care of her ... being so mad and helpless. I thought she could be the child I haven't had so far ... the sister I've never had or the friend who went away. I would bathe her every day, we'd play together ... but he said no. He said, after you've dressed her and fed her, you send her back to where she came from ... she's dangerous, he said ... madwomen are dangerous ... You can't keep a madwoman in my house, in our house. I felt so sad." She let out a long weary sigh. "He also told me not to venture out into the streets again, it was not safe there, with madwoman roaming all over."

Oddly, the old woman didn't comment on that, she only said, "I'll massage your legs now."

"I dressed her up. It was like dressing a child ... or a doll. I dressed her in some of my best clothes. He didn't object, he was so anxious to get rid of her. I think – I think he was scared. She laughed loudly, laughed like a madwoman when I put on those clothes, stroked my silk sari, put it against her cheek. Then I gave her some food. She didn't know how to eat, I had to feed her with a spoon like you feed a baby. Can you imagine anyone so helpless? And then – I led her out of the door and into the street – I led her by the hand like a child and left her on the street – my dream madwoman. And when she stood there looking at me with her big, wild eyes – I wanted to cry ..."

"You wanted to cry ..."

"But I didn't cry," the young woman's eyes were big and wild now. "I didn't want him to see me cry. I crept inside ... but I wanted to look at her once again before she disappeared ... so I peeped out of the window. And what do you think I saw?"

"What did you see?"

"I saw her tearing off the clothes I'd dressed her in. She tore up my lovely silk sari, the matching blouse and petticoat and she tore off the lovely bras and panties I'd put on her, the ones he bought on his last trip abroad. And then she picked up the old blanket from the side of the road where I,d thrown it, and put it around her and went away. She didn't turn around to look at me even once ... not even once. I was about to run out of the house after her but then ... I woke up ..."

Then she turned around to look into the old woman's eyes. "Do *you* think this dream was sent to me to save my life?" Her voice was mocking.

"Maybe, maybe, there is much we cannot understand," the old woman looked confused now – as if she'd thought that she knew everything but wasn't so sure now. 'But ... perhaps it'll take you some time to find out."

A loud shriek startled her. It was the young woman, Ketaki. She was tearing off – no she was tearing up her clothes. She had already taken them off for the massage.

"Hush," said the old woman. "Hush ..." She held the young woman's arms tightly till she stopped struggling, gave up exhausted. Then she cradled her in her arms. The young woman buried her head in her lap and moaned and whimpered, "I lied to you, I lied to you ... it was not an incomplete dream ... I didn't tell you the end ... because there was an end ... I ran after her and when she turned around, I saw that her face had changed ... she looked just like me ... no, she had become me – or I had become her!"

The old woman's hands were very soft now – as soft as silk. "It doesn't matter," she said, "It doesn't matter. It was just a dream ..." In a lower voice she said, "But remember what your husband said ... never venture outside these safe walls. You might bring a madwoman from the streets into your house ... and find yourself!"

ICARUS REBORN

Unexpectedly, the nagging drizzle that had compelled Sanjay Pal to keep his windshield wipers moving turned into a downpour. Driving like an automaton through the dense traffic, he watched the battle between the rain and the wipers with a whimsical eye. The drops pouring down ceaselessly and the wiper frantically erasing them, only to find them fogging the windshield again. Who would win? The rain called the shots, obviously. The wipers were compelled to keep on the move while it was there. They could only rest when it decided to withdraw.

But the rain didn't stop even when he reached the hotel where the meeting was being held. Not that it created a problem. He would drive into the portico and hand the keys to the waiting flunkey. The car would be valet parked and he would step into the hotel, natty and self-possessed. Even the downpour couldn't wash away the image he had so assiduously created, the imposing edifice built brick by brick over so many years.

Sanjay Pal was well prepared for the meeting. He had no anxieties at all – it would be a pushover. Because the simple truth was – he was at his peak and flying high.

He was repeating the opening words of his little speech in his mind again – he never took chances – as he stepped into the lift. At that very moment his eyes – in the wanton way your senses sometimes take off on their own, reached through the fast closing doors to alight on a woman.

A woman dressed in a bright pink sari.

Something fluttered in his brain, minuscule wings carrying him away to another time or windscreen wipers frantically clearing a lucid space in the fog of memory. Sunanda. His heart flopped about like a clumsy fish. Helplessly he watched his hand rising, reaching out to press the button – but the lift was already climbing upwards. The dampness spread on his brow as he watched the numbers materializing above the door with a kind of sick desperation. The moment it stopped he elbowed his way out, ignoring the astonished, even outraged glances the other occupants hurled at him.

A suited booted neck tied man behaving like a proper junglee.

But he was oblivious to their thoughts and too impatient to wait for the other lift to come down and leapt down the stairs two at a time. Back in the lobby, which seemed to have become more crowded in the space of those brief moments, his eyes scrambled over faces rejecting them one by one as his disappointment escalated. Please God, she couldn't have gone, vanished in those few minutes. Or had he been hallucinating?

No, it was not possible.

He took a deep breath and resurrected that cool methodical self, which had suddenly gone underground and made his eyes travel slowly through the lobby from one end to the other.

He found her.

Seated primly in a corner almost hidden behind the lush bank of foliage that stretched above the sofa she was occupying. He paused for a moment before accosting her – it was her, still recognizable despite the passage of time and its attendant ravages. He took note of the fullness of her figure and the fact that she hadn't bothered to dye her hair. It could be deliberate. The grey hair set off the large bindi effectively, her heavily kaajaled eyes and the bright pink sari that had attracted his attention. She was a woman he would have noticed even if she hadn't been Sunanda.

He could already feel the corners of his mouth stretching. The smile that crouched there leapt up like a dizzy gazelle.

"Sunanda!" he tried to make the exclamation sound natural. His heart flung a painful blow at his chest when she turned, frowning.

The moisture beading his brow spread to the corners of his eyes. Maybe he should have paused for a moment, not been so impetuous. Maybe he should have approached her with a polite, "Excuse me," instead of springing on her like a maniac.

Then, miraculously, the lines smoothed away. "You?" she said with incredulous accusation.

"How-how are you?" he clutched at the clichéd opening. "I

caught a glimpse of you as I was passing … and said … that looks like Sunanda."

A thought of the meeting which was about to begin in the next few minutes flickered in his mind like a feeble beacon, then died. "How are you?" he asked again, to distract himself from the sight of that painfully familiar smile.

"You've already asked me," she pointed out.

"But you didn't reply." His mind had freed itself from the paralysis her presence had clamped on it.

"Very well, thank you."

The force that possessed him gave him the strength to ignore her mockery. "What are you doing here?" The question sounded presumptuous, almost rude. He had no right to ask it, in that demanding way.

But she didn't take it amiss. "Waiting," she said simply. "For my husband ... You've grown fat." Accusing him again.

"It's thirty years," he said, then stopped.

For a moment they gazed at each other as if trying to fit each other into the present, this moment so far removed from the others, that existed so long ago.

Then unexpectedly she said, "Do you remember that time, when you conned me into believing that you could actually fly? That you knew a magic mantra? How gullible I was!" Her laughter still had a girlish spontaneity. He opened his mouth to reply, then stopped again as a sharp nostalgia gripped him, so sharp that it made his eyes burn.

Sunanda was six, he an all knowing eight year old. They lived in houses planted side by side in the midst of a row of cement blocks that stretched on and on till they ended abruptly in a vast open space. As if the houses felt they had grown far enough and it was time to stop. It was not one of those so-called parks that relieve the monotony of planned housing colonies in large cities, provide lungs for choked urban chests. Just a maidan covered with scattered grass and the debris of human existence. An abandoned neglected piece of earth but all the same, a good place to fly kites, or just race about feeling the wind in your face, working off that tightness coiled inside which made you want to jump and jump till it loosened itself and set you free. Perhaps he had been doing just that that day and the strong current of air pushing at his body made him feel he was actually flying.

"Come on, I'm going to make you fly!" he'd told Sunanda, grabbing her hand.

She was scared at first but perhaps the thought became appealing when he said, "Don't you want to be like a bird? They can go wherever they want … Come on, close your eyes, where do you want to go?"

"I don't know." Fear had cramped her voice.

"All right, I'll take you to Vilayat."

"Vilayat?" He realized the word didn't mean anything to her and she had agreed because he was Sanjay bhaiya who lived next door and knew so much more than her.

He had raced along the maidan with her, picking up speed, almost dragging her along, then hoisted her up and flung her into the air. "I'm flying," she cried, full of astonished delight.

He tried to catch her when she fell but could only break her fall, tumbling down with her onto the dry, wispy grass. She had cut her leg on a piece of tin left carelessly on the maidan. The scolding he got had bothered him more than her outraged howls, "You lied! You lied! You don't know how to fly!"

If she hadn't got hurt, he might have died laughing.

"So, have you learnt to fly now?"

"You have an amazing memory," he said sheepishly. What a silly trick, couldn't he have done better? Why did she have to bring this up? "Do you go back there ever?"

She shook her head. "My father died many years ago. My mother lives with my younger brother, sometimes with me."

He could remember her mother. Sunanda had inherited that pearly complexion, much admired in their neighbourhood, from her, also that direct, wide-open glance, the full mobile mouth. That was how he had recognized her at once, she looked so much like her mother as he remembered her. Maya mausi, he had called her and she spent much time at their place assisting his mother in the making of pickles in summer during the mango season and sitting with her in the sun and knitting on balmy winter afternoons. She had been doing just that when he brought a bleeding Sunanda home. He experienced the force of his mother's hand as never before that day, and for a short while Sunanda stopped playing with him.

But that was not his most potent memory of her. It was something that had happened much later, when he was eighteen, the day before he was leaving for engineering college. An event so important in their neighbourhood that a large group of people came to the station to see him off. Sunanda was not among them, she had already said good-bye the evening before.

He was in his room, the little cell on the terrace that he occupied, because he needed privacy to study, as he said, but actually to get away from his father. Because ever since his voice had deepened and he had begun to use a razor, his father's speeches on the 'art of living wisely' had assumed intolerable proportions. Being a teacher in the local government school, used to scattering pearls of wisdom at random before his students, cheerfully oblivious to the fact that no one was bothering to pick them up, he felt that his son should not be denied the benefits he handed out so freely to others.

He heard someone rattling the iron chain on their front door, very few people had door bells then. His father considered it a pompous extravagance. From the sound, short, staccato, he guessed it was Sunanda. She had outgrown her gullible babyhood to turn into a sharp, edgy girl who would chop your pretensions away pitilessly without a second thought. He guessed too, that she must have come to say good-bye. After all they had known each other for sixteen years. It made it quite easy to predict how the other would act.

Or so he thought.

There was nothing sentimental about that leave taking. They shared a jocular, easy going, brother-sister type relationship. So much so that neither of their parents felt they needed to be on guard where the two of them were concerned. He was truly an honorary older brother, she even tied rakhis on him.

"Don't let us down," she said gravely, loading him with an uneasy weight, more expectations added to those of his parents. He felt mildly disappointed, he expected her to keep this heavy moment light hearted, if no one else did. She put a small wrapped up cardboard box into his hand. He could guess what it would be again. A pen set. It was the type of gift people in their neighbourhood would give someone going off as he was, to college. He got at least five pen sets and was compelled to acknowledge later that they were appropriate and useful presents. There was also an envelope along with it. He could guess what it must be too. A good luck card painted by her. She had always been fond of painting and birthdays and the approach of examinations meant that she would present him with delicate water colours of flowers or birds twining upwards to a message saying 'Happy Birthday' or 'Good Luck' as the occasion might be. She would also have strong objections if she didn't display these cards for an appropriate length of time in his room. It made him smile, though his throat thickened thinking of this card displayed in that faraway room he was yet to see.

He was about to open the envelope, when she said, "You can see it later," smiling mysteriously as if it was a masterpiece which had to be perused in private for full effect.

"I'll write to you," he said. Suddenly the enormity of the experience he was about to undergo burst on him. Leave home, face the rigours of some alien, possibly hostile place. Live amongst strangers. Panic overwhelmed him. He had seldom traveled far from his hometown apart from the routine journeys with his parents to visit relatives, attend family weddings which could not be bypassed. These too were few and far between, his father's finances didn't permit it. As such his education at the engineering college was a major expense. But Pitaji had taken it on cheerfully as an investment in his future.

He stood there frozen, watching an unexpected gleam spark in Sunanda's eyes as he said that.

It was a muggy oppressive July evening and the bitter odour of putrefying neem fruit hung in the air. In contrast, she looked freshly washed, with the smell of soap and talc strong on her. He couldn't smile as he said good-bye, brushing her eyes with his, finding nothing in her neutral gaze. Brother and sister they might be considered but in those times physical contact with a girl was unthinkable. Especially for him. His father's lectures had seeped through despite everything.

He had discovered the envelope later, unpacking his tin trunk in the room that had been allotted to him. Aching with the sense of loss, which pursued him all the way, through the lonely train journey to the confusion wrought progress to the hostel in a rickshaw. Then the numb terror of beholding the huge grey anonymous structure that towered above him and hearing excluding laughter all around him. He smiled in anticipation, at the thought of the card he would put up on the scratched wooden table that would serve as his desk.

But Sunanda had not made a card for him. The envelope

contained a photograph – hers. Confounded, he stared at it as if the flat, black and white reproduction of her smiling face could provide an answer. Why had she done that? He was fond of her but it had not occurred to him to carry photographs of his parents or even his older brother, working in a far away city, who had been the one to put the idea of trying for admission to the engineering college in his head. They were not the type of people who put up photographs in their homes. Of dead ancestors of course, duly garlanded. Or class groups, their sepia tones blending into dusty walls. Maybe when his brother got married, one of the bridal couple would appear. But right now, none other. He turned it over to see if there was a message behind it. There was none. The sound of approaching footsteps made him push it into a book.

Suddenly it made him feel shy.

The photograph returned to trouble him during the next few days whenever his thoughts could take a brief respite from the bludgeoning confusion that surrounded him like a numbing fog. The strangeness of his surroundings, the nauseous food, the new routine and – the ragging. It had been a month before he recalled his promise to write to Sunanda, and only when his mother mentioned in a letter that she had been asking about him. But when he sat down to write, he was afraid to ask why she had given him her photograph.

He ended up penning a bland, almost dull account of his new life, omitting the pain, the terror and the sheer exhaustion that filled his days. Though there were times (when his roommate was not around) when he would take out the photograph to gaze at it, as if it could offer a clue to what had become an insoluble mystery. Sometimes, it looked alien, a stranger's photograph. He had never seen Sunanda smile like that, she looked provocative, almost sexy. He felt bashful, blushed when these words crept like interlopers across the surface of his mind, overturning his memories of Sunanda, uncovering some dark, unfathomable current. There were times when he felt like tearing it up, it troubled him so much, but in the end, he could never bear to.

It was Varun, wandering into his room in his casual way, who exposed him. The relationship he formed with that group of boys was something between the expediency born of circumstance and extreme emotional need. He had to ally himself with someone, be part of some group, he was not a loner by nature. He needed someone to hang out with in the evenings, share raucous conversation with at meal times, discuss studies or films – anything at all. Varun was all right. He liked to get his way but would support you against anyone. Sanjay felt he was lucky that he had sought him out. Along with his roommate Niraj, and classmates Rakesh and Sumit they formed a tidy group.

In his fidgety way, Varun had been playing with the things on his desk. His pens, his notebooks, letters from his parents, other mundane objects scattered about in the usual state of disarray. When he picked up the book in which he had hidden the photograph, began to ruffle the pages, Sanjay looked away, out of the window. A wheeling bird suspended itself in the sky even as he watched.

He could have grabbed the photograph and run, turned it

into a joke, thrown it out of the window. But overcome by confusion as he was, he let himself solidify into an unwieldy rock.

When Varun whistled, he experienced a weary sense of deja vous. "Quite a cheez! Who is she? Don't pretend it's your sister. Quite a guy you are! Who would imagine it, looking at you!"

In the clamour that followed, with everyone grabbing at Sunanda's photograph, he felt himself expand. The look Varun threw at him, admiration and envy combined into a heady mixture, exploded in his head with potent force.

For a few days, he was almost an object of awe. At that age, eighteen and in that era of segregation of the sexes, hardly any of them could brag of a girl friend. A girl who actually existed, in a real flesh and blood relationship. All they had were the pinups that plastered the walls of their rooms and their fantasies.

Sanjay wasn't sure when Sunanda became one of the pinups. When envy overtook admiration and his so-called romance was sacrificed at the altar of camaraderie. He should have guessed when Niraj brought a frame and said, "Yaar, you don't have to hide her away. Put her up on your desk where she belongs."

Amused, a little chagrined, he had agreed. He was not sure whether to blame Sunanda or bless her for giving him this photograph. But a vague discomfort was beginning to stir in him. This thing was growing, acquiring dimensions he could hardly have expected. It was not a joke any longer.

Could it have been ignorance that prevented him from reacting to Varun's remark, a few days later?

It was that hour of night, post dinner and the stroll around the compound, when the oppressive air drove them into their rooms. An hour when forced proximity, sheer boredom sometimes, compelled souls to bare themselves. "So – how is it between you two – just writing poetry – or some real action? Somehow, yaar, you don't look the type who would write poetry." His narrow, glittering gaze fixed Sanjay.

It took him more than a moment to comprehend, forcing Niraj to drive the point home by saying, "Come on, yaar, don't look so innocent. I'm sure there's plenty going on. Come on – we're all pals here together."

He felt the silence in the room like the hot, fetid breath of an uncaged monster, a monster that needed to be fed. But there was also the exhilarating recognition of the image he had acquired via Sunanda's photograph. The image that wiped out the existence of his unfashionable, even shabby clothes, his inability to throw around money like Varun or Rakesh could. He was being given an opportunity to redeem himself, even assume a position of importance in the gang.

It was not very hard to feed the monster, to create a Sanjay who was an indefatigable fornicator, a Sunanda who had an insatiable appetite. His own ability to pluck out lurid scenarios, give form and substance to airy nothing astonished him. So convincingly that the time came when fact and fiction grew so muddled in his mind that he found it hard to believe that these things had not really happened. How could they not have happened? Surely they had hurried, stolen sex standing up in his room when they could not restrain the urge? Surely she sneaked out over her terrace at night to join him? Surely her breasts were like ripening mangoes and she had a mole on the lower part of her belly?

The confusion became so great that he had to stop writing to Sunanda, tell her that he was too busy to correspond. There was also the fear that one of her letters might be intercepted and he be exposed when their pitiful contents were made public.

Then the first vacation came around and he experienced a sudden, overpowering terror. How would he face Sunanda, stand being in the same room as her? Suppose his own fictions overpowered him so that he could not stop himself from living them. Ultimately he told his parents he could not come home, he had to study. There was also the matter of the expense. They were disappointed but proud of his resolve.

He did get puzzled looks from his friends. "Aren't you dying to get back together with her?"

His agile mind came up with a convincing answer. "The bitch is getting married," he said. "To someone else. My mother wrote. I don't want to go home!" He turned away as if to hide his agony.

Their sympathy was overwhelming. To the extent that Varun suggested getting even with her by informing her husband to be about their relationship.

For a moment Sanjay felt real fear. Was the monster about to escape, unleash the terror he was struggling to rein in? But again he had been able to rescue himself. "Forget it, yaar. I'm sure her parents forced her. Her father's the kind." He sighed and smiled sadly. "I'm going to write to her and wish her good luck. How could she have waited for me? It'll take a long, long time for me to get settled."

They had all nodded in understanding. They knew what a long haul they had ahead of them before they could even contemplate marriage.

Varun looked at him as if he was recognizing him for what he was for the first time. And Niraj put a consoling arm around his shoulder. "Yaar, are you sure, you're going to be okay alone?"

"Don't worry," he replied. "Actually … I'm glad not to have this distraction around. I can concentrate on my studies now."

It left them speechless.

When his friends came back, Sunanda was past history for them. But not for him, because the wedding card actually arrived. Because Sunanda did get married, nine months after he last saw her, when she gave him that photograph. Perhaps it was the memory of his father's lectures that was responsible for the letter he forced himself to write, full of trite clichés, laden with false sentiments. He knew they were false because he had realized, he was not sure at which particular moment of that soul-searing, gut wrenching ordeal what he really felt about her.

In the next vacation his mother told him that she had made a brilliant marriage and had gone abroad with her husband. And a couple of years later his father retired and moved away to live with his brother.

Sunanda's eyes turned away to fix themselves on a man approaching them. A little older than Sanjay, dressed in a kurta-pajama. So she hangs out with these arty crafty types, he thought. Resentment surged. Why didn't he know what had happened to her in the space of these thirty years? Why couldn't he ask her why she had given him her photograph?

The man came right up to them. "Rahul," she said. "This is Sanjay, my childhood friend. Remember? That lovely letter I showed you when we got married. He was the one who wrote it."

"Oh yes," the grey bearded man's face brightened. "I've heard a lot about you."

"Nothing bad I hope." Was the tremor in his voice noticeable?

"Keep guessing." It was Sunanda who replied. " I think I still have your letter somewhere. So nice to see you, Sanjay. After all these years."

The meeting went off well. He wasn't late, the rain held the others up. But when he came out, it had been replaced by a breeze so strong that it almost blew him away as he stood on the steps of the hotel lobby, waiting for his car. Funny, he thought, that of all the memories they had shared she should recall that particular one so vividly.

DOORWAYS WITHOUT DOORS

It stood halfway down the hill, just next to the spring which was supposed to have the best drinking water in the whole area. Not really a house, just a long narrow structure. A row of rooms with arched doorways – doorways without doors. Utterly decrepit, black with a coating of ancient moss, shelter for the poorest of the poor – a dharamshala.

Cactus sprouted from its roof, rampant, unchecked, stretched prickly arms to the sky. An old tun tree spread benevolent branches over it, added its own soft cover of fallen leaves to the carpet of moss that luxuriated atop the stolid slate roof.

Pragya wasn't sure why she had been so eager to come here. It had not been easy. Someone had blocked the old path that led down to the dharamshala from her house with thorns. Typically, it strengthened her determination, she had to get here at any cost. She had edged around the barrier, scrambled down an uneven slope, clutching at tufts of grass that provided a dangerously fragile hold, getting pierced with the very thorns she was trying to avoid and scraping a knee despite the frail protection of her cotton salwar.

On hindsight, it seemed rather silly to adopt this costume if she had made up her mind to go slipping and sliding down the hillside, rather than a more practical pair of jeans. But she was sensitive to the stares it might have provoked in this little town, unused to the sight of middle-aged women in pants, even though she chided herself for being a coward. Why couldn't she wear the clothes she had been wearing regularly for the last sixteen years? Why should coming home mean shrinking behind this flimsy armour?

But again, what compelled her to come scrambling down this impossible path? Nostalgia, a desire to get away from the sick room atmosphere, or just plain restlessness? Mamma had dozed off, there was a competent person attending to her – Abha – more competent than she was perhaps, so she needn't feel guilty about taking a short walk, she had told herself firmly as she set off with the brittle April breeze stroking hercheeks. The pines murmured, imitating the music a sluggish rivulet might make. A sound so deceptive that it often induced visitors new to the place to enquire where the stream that they heard was flowing. The translucent warmth of the sunshine tempered the wind and despite the anxiety, the ennui of the past week, she experienced a sudden elation.

As a child she had sometimes come down here with her ayah for walks, or accompanied a servant to fetch water when the municipal supply let them down.

She found the place strange and curious then and would often hang back to peer into the ever open doorways, scanning the darkness that prowled behind them, inhaling the peculiar odour that emanated from within. A compost of animal dung, scorched rice and damp, along with a generous hint of stale tobacco and unwashed bodies. Sometimes she would find an itinerant sadhu camped here, his eyes rolling redly, his matted locks inducing a strange prickling at the ends of her fingers as he puffed at his clay hookah. Only the fear of her ayah prevented her from going closer to touch them. More often, there would be a group of dotiyals, men from the north who worked as porters, dressed frugally in sackcloth with round caps perched on their heads. Sometimes muleteers stopped here for a night. They were responsible for the earthy odour of mule dung, which had become a permanent presence.

"Come on!" her ayah would admonish, her tough palms scraping Pragya's hand as she pulled her away. Pragya's fascination for this dilapidated place seemed to bother her. As if her charge of this middle class child entailed keeping her away from such sights, apart from more clearly defined duties like bathing her, changing her clothes, taming her coarse, thick hair to make it lie flat and sleek on her small head, fetching the glass of milk to be drunk morning and evening. She would only agree to come down here when Pragya fussed so much in the course of the mandatory evening walk that she feared denial might result in an unpleasant scene; which could lead to adverse reports being passed on to Pragya's mother by inquisitive passers-by, this being a place where everyone knew everyone else.

But at a certain stage of her life, the ayah had left and as other forces intervened, the fascination had worn off, even though Pragya couldn't help glancing at the place curiously if she should ever happen to pass this way.

Some things had changed. The old house with the caved in roof that used to perch on the slope overlooking the spring had disappeared. It had been replaced by a garish cemented edifice painted in unlikely shades of blue and green that clashed violently with both the sky overhead and the faded grass of the hillside behind it. She remembered the story, extracted piecemeal from her reluctant ayah and further embellished by another more willing servant. The story of the woman who had once occupied that house, the do gooder who constructed the dharamshala, a rani.

"Whose house is this?" She had asked the ayah, pointing at the dharamshala, the first time she brought her down here, a mistake Pragya knew she always regretted.

"Nobody's – everybody's," the old woman had said. Her face was crisscrossed with as many wrinkles as the narrow paths that scored the hillside above and she smelled of the bidis she smoked surreptitiously.

"Is that why there are no doors?" Pragya asked. "So that anyone can go in?"

"Yes," the ayah nodded, playing along. At that time it seemed like a welcome distraction for this troublesome child, who wanted to run about here and there, leaving little time for the ayah to sit down and smoke her bidi in peace. "If there were doors then there would be locks and everyone could not come and stay here. Only those who had keys."

"But someone must have built it for everyone to stay here," Pragya asked. "Who?"

"A rani," the ayah said. At that time she had been quite willing to talk about this place. It was before Pragya's obsession with it had begun to trouble her.

"A rani? Built this? This broken down old house for everyone?" She had been disbelieving. What kind of queen would build something like this? A queen would build a palace – something grand.

"You're telling lies. You've made it up! I don't believe you!"

"It's true!" The ayah's tone matched hers. Sometimes they squabbled on an equal footing. Sometimes Pragya pushed her advantage, that of class and sometimes the ayah pushed hers, that of age. "It wasn't broken down when she built it. She built it so that poor travellers could have a place to stay."

"But why?"

"She wanted to perform a good deed. And now we're going home, it's getting dark. Your mother will get angry." She had grabbed Pragya's hand and pulled her up the hill.

It was the servant who provided the rest of the story. He was not directly responsible for Pragya and when she followed him down to fetch water it was because no one else wanted to deal with her tantrums, finding it easier to let her have her way. So he did not bother to consider the consequences of answering the stream of questions that flowed from her like the ayah did.

"Why did the rani build the house for travellers? Why did she want to do a good deed?" She had been watching the water trickle down from the spring, tamed into a channel, into the bucket, filling it soundlessly. The sun was strong that day and the stone enclosure which covered the spring, this water source that flowed eternally and never dried up, even during the hottest of summers, felt deliciously cool. Quivering rods of sunlight executed a playful dance on its grey mossy walls and the damp air soothed her heated cheeks.

The servant had laughed. He had a soft full laugh which turned his eyes into slits, made his black moustache quiver. Then he sobered up suddenly. "Because she was sick … very sick … she thought if she did a good deed she would get cured."

"How silly! You can't get cured by good deeds," she shot back at once. "You have to go to the doctor if you're sick and take medicine."

"Sometimes good deeds also help," the man said shortly. "And now we must go back because I have to cook lunch."

She had paused to glance back at the house with its caved in roof and fired one last question at him as she scrambled up the slope. "Did she get all right?"

The man paused too, before answering. "I don't know."

Somehow she had guessed that he was lying. Even then it had annoyed her that someone should try to fool her with stories, though beneath that annoyance an odd hope had lingered, that it could be possible. That good deeds could cure diseases or effect other miracles. Later, when she was much older, had totally lost interest in that dharamshala or anything else like it, she had once heard her mother tell a visitor about the spring, which gave the area its name and the tubercular queen who eventually succumbed to her illness, despite all her good deeds. It was just another story, like the others that sprouted like grass on the hillside in her hometown.

It was just a few years before she met Vinay. She was in college at that time and the rani's story had not invoked much interest then; just that faint flicker which the answer to an old riddle might stir up. An answer that doesn't seem relevant any more because curiosity has evaporated long ago, been replaced by disinterest. At the most it provoked amusement at naïveté of this kind. She was living in a hostel in a big city then and had acquired all kinds of new knowledge and experience, far beyond what had been available to her in this little town. Visits home passed in a haze of ennui, which felt like a suspension of time that was spending itself despite the fact that everything seemed to be standing still. Time that progressed just because clocks and calendars decreed it must rather than any effort on her part to move it along. Her father, her beloved Papa was still alive then but her older brother Saurabh had not got married. That event would take place the following year and her father pass away two years later, just when she was on the verge of completing her studies.

Papa's death had changed many things. She learned to be afraid of the unexpected, an element of uncertainty crept into that rather smug existence of hers. It had brought first disbelief, then anger that some force on which she had relied with such surety had suddenly withdrawn its favour from her, treated her like anyone else and finally implanted that fear into her heart. The fear which never left her for the rest of her life. Later it brought on the uncomfortable realisation that no one would be around to indulge her whims now, something she had begun to believe was her birthright. Her father indulged her so much that she took her status as a privileged being for granted. Someone who was special, born to be loved and have every wish fulfilled. Suddenly life came into brutal focus and she realized that she would have to take on another role, or rather experience a reversal of roles, be a kind of parent to the parent who remained, her mother, who had collapsed into a state of utter helplessness. She would be compelled to cosset Mamma's grief because her older brother had no interest in doing so, and despite her youth, her immaturity, slowly pamper, nurse it into a state of acceptance. But also into a state in which she, Pragya, became an essential prop to Mamma's existence.

When Vinay appeared on the scene he appeared to be the ally she badly needed in the mission to maintain her mother's well being. The thought of a lifelong bulwark was so appealing that she surrendered to it right away. People had been surprised when she announced her engagement. Vinay was short, dark and beginning to show signs of a paunch at the age of twenty-seven. Too much of a contrast to what people described as her ethereal beauty, despite his excellent qualifications as an engineer from a premier institute. But Mamma and Saurabh were relieved. Because Vinay was so completely smitten that he was satisfied with the simplest of weddings, all they could afford at the time. And her confidence in this infatuation made it easy for her to disregard the displeasure, the coldness from the in-laws who felt cheated. There was someone who would indulge her again, like her father and this belief gave her the strength to shore her mother up.

She didn't know at the time that the process of change that had set in with her father's death was still in motion. She realized it only when Vinay came and told her that he had made plans to leave the country. Without even consulting her. He had not thought it would be necessary, he was the decision maker and she the person who deferred to his decisions. It was only then that she realized that this bulwark was a wall built from her own illusions, her own needs.

"But your brother is there to take care of your mother," he had said, bewildered at her protests. "And you can visit whenever our finances permit."

She stared at him dumbfounded, blinking back her tears, trying to make sense of his words. They had been married for more than a year, seventeen months to be exact. Shweta was just three months old. Her married life had so far followed the established pattern. The wedding, the honeymoon, the new house, furnishing which had been like creating the backdrop to an enchanted dream. And then the baby, the plump pretty daughter who, everyone had declared with approval, looked just like the mother. And now this, this incomprehensible decision to uproot them all, take them to an alien place, far from all she cherished. How long had he been plotting and planning behind her back?

"But-but, why do we need to go?" she had asked. It was evening, that treasured time of day when he returned from office, weary but fulfilled. Another day of work, more money earned to keep his family in comfort, more security for them all. The time when he savoured his rewards, his blessings – playing with the baby, being pampered by Pragya. She had just served him a plate of hot onion pakoras, his favorites, when he asked her to turn off the gas and sit down. She misunderstood, thought it was love, an overwhelming desire for her company, which compelled him to make this request. She smiled and sat down on the sofa next to him, reached for his hand. Shweta was lying on a mattress on the floor, kicking her legs blissfully. Perhaps the fact that his responding smile was so fleeting should have alerted her.

At first she was not sure she heard right. He had to repeat it again; "I've got admission in a university in the U.S. to do my Ph.D. I'm getting full financial support." He had drawn a long, quivering breath and looked at her with shining eyes.

It had taken a few minutes for the words to register. Her first reaction was to quickly pull her hand away. "You-you mean to say, you're leaving us, going away?" Tears streamed from her eyes.

"No, silly," he grabbed her hand and squeezed it. "How can I leave you? You'll join me later, as soon as I'm a little settled."

"But-but, why do we need to go?"

"For a better future for us all."

"But you never told me!" The words came out in a kind of

wail, instead of the protest that she intended them to be.

He was silent for a moment. "I wasn't sure it would work out. Didn't want to tell you till it was final."

It did not take her long to realize how final it was. That the man who she had believed would be puttee in her hands had an agenda of his own, had already had it when he met her. That what she believed was her duty to her mother did not enter into it, because he couldn't recognize it as such.

She had spent the eight months it had taken for him to get settled with Mamma, stoutly resisting her mother-in-law's commands that she come and stay with her. It was a form of revenge against Vinay.

All the same Mamma hadn't bothered to conceal the feeling of betrayal she experienced. Paradoxically, her reproaches, her nagging, made it easier for her to leave when the time came. The initial feelings of sorrow and guilt hardened into resentment. Why couldn't Mamma understand? Later she wasn't so sure. Was it the same resentment, which turned against Vinay later when he decided that he was not going to come home and work as he had said earlier? But she had come to terms with the facts of her existence and learned to rein in such feelings.

By that time Abha had become firmly established with Mamma, the fourteen-year-old girl she had installed as a companion, helper, surrogate daughter, whatever.

Saurabh and she had made a bargain. Mamma would spend winter with him. She would provide financial support to make her life more comfortable. Vinay had agreed to it. It was the bargain she made with him in turn, so that their lives could retain some semblance of their earlier wedded bliss. Later she had been able to send tickets for Mamma to visit when she herself couldn't, because after a time she too had found a job, created her own bulwark, a real one.

Mamma has been cared for, Pragya thinks, contemplating the doorless doorways of the dharamshala. She has even been able to transform a girl's life. Abha, the daughter of a drunken carpenter has had the opportunity to go to school, to college, now even holds a well-paid job as a teacher, well-paid enough for her. She hasn't married, of course. If she had, who would have looked after Mamma? Saurabh's wife could not take on the responsibility. Mamma could be cantankerous, her demands were impossible to fulfill, even the three months that fell to Saurabh's lot were a burden too great for them to bear. Luckily Abha, being a teacher, had holidays for part of those three months, even though Lata found it distasteful that she should use the guest room along with Mamma. But where else could she sleep? And what if Mamma needed something at night? Lata certainly didn't care to be disturbed.

And then, who would have married Abha? She had grown out of her class, would be hard put to adjust to someone of say, her father's level.

But now, Mamma's dying. Pragya knows that, hears it in the groans that keep her awake all night. Sometimes she sits up on her bed, her heart thumping uneasily. Is it coming, that awful moment? Sometimes she falls into an uneasy sleep in which Mamma's spirit seems to waft around her touching her with vaporous fingers, cold as the mist outside. She awakes with a start to hear Mamma groaning again and is not sure if she should be relieved that her life drags on, however painfully. She wonders if she should go and see if she needs anything. Sometimes she does, only to see Abha seated there, bony faced, silent, shaking her head when she asks if anything is required of her. Mamma does not groan all the time. Sometimes she seems to be delirious, reliving the past. She even repeats the story of the rani who died despite her battle, the ineffectual artillery of good works she had employed against death.

The story doesn't matter. There's a new twist that she discovered last night, though, through Mamma's ramblings. That the rani was young and beautiful and longed to live, was desperate to live. Does Mamma want to live, even though she keeps praying for deliverance? Is her life precious enough for her, lonely and neglected though she may consider herself? And unexpectedly, another thought intrudes. If deliverance should come ... what about Abha, what'll happen to her? The thirty-year-old schoolteacher who gravely performs her duty. The duty of which she will soon be relieved.

Sometimes she finds her in tears, this rather grim looking young woman. She has performed her duty well, all these years, developed a genuine attachment to Mamma, despite those demands which had grown more and more difficult to fulfill as age and infirmity took their toll. There have been times that Pragya has argued with herself, wondering if she should be paid for these services. Saurabh feels that what Mamma has done is more than enough. Food, shelter, clothes education ... could any other girl of her class have hoped to achieve what she has without Mamma's help? It's obvious Abha feels her position is above that of a servant's. A few years ago she stubbornly refused the tips Pragya tried to hand to her at the end of her yearly visit. After a couple of tries Pragya learned to substitute what she thought were reasonably decent gifts as part payment for the debt she sometimes feels she owes the girl. Even though she knows it's not her fault she could not take care of her mother the way she should have. Even though Saurabh is not conscious of any such lapse, she is fulfilling her part of the bargain as he is. But Pragya lies awake at night subjecting herself to the torture of self castigation. Hadn't Mamma been emotionally dependent on her? Can financial security stand in for the presence of a loved one, a child in one's old age? These are questions to which she can never find answers.

"If there had been doors, people would have been shut out ..."

"What doors? What are you talking about?" Saurabh looks irritable.

Mamma's dead, the funeral's over. Now it's time to settle all those other mundane matters, tie up the loose ends left behind after someone's death. Earthly possessions, clothes, furniture, property.

They sit in the verandah despite the evening chill, at her insistence. Inside, Mamma's missing presence is too strong. Saurabh has agreed despite the fact that his wife has a cold. Perhaps because he's afraid inside Abha might eavesdrop. So they sit and watch the darkness congeal around them, braving the assaults the coming of night inflicts on them.

As Pragya makes her reply, Lata draws her shawl around her and sighs. "I'm talking about the dharamshala down below, near the spring."

Saurabh clicks his tongue. Saurabh, five years older, who had already gone away to boarding school when she negotiated that rocky path with her ayah. "What does that have to do with us?"

"What dharamshala?" Lata asks peevishly. Pragya knows how much she resents not being a part of their shared past, would blot it out totally if it were possible. Perhaps she'll manage to, now that Mamma's gone.

"Nothing really, perhaps," Pragya delights in ignoring her. "My mind was just wandering. Actually Mamma's mind wandered a lot lately. She was talking about the rani, the one who had built the dharamshala and died of tuberculosis ... Sorry," she sat up straight. "I shouldn't digress. Yes, we have to decide what to do with the house, since neither of us is likely to come here much again."

She felt a pang as she said this, seemed to hear a door slam which shouldn't have, a door that shut her out from something that had once been important to her life. But that was the way it had always been. Doors closing on compartments of her life, which sealed themselves up to become part of the jumbled storehouse of memory. Pathways blocked off with thorns. And soon she'd be hard put to scramble down that path again, stand face to face with the powerless magic of good deeds.

Powerless ... Could it be called magic if it had no power? She thought of the rani . . . she hadn't really died as everyone believed but lived in the mossy walls of the dharamshala, floated in and out of the doorless doorways, along with the travellers who camped there. It was her scent she had been searching for so long ago, the scent of the person who constructed a shelter, however poor and decrepit.

No, death wasn't really a door slamming as she had thought.

"Yes, the house," she repeated. "I want to give my share to Abha. That's what Mamma would have wanted, wouldn't she? She did take on our burden." She looked straight into Saurabh's eyes as she said this, which dropped, to his credit. "Perhaps she'll let me come and stay here sometimes ... And now I think I'll go inside," she added, looking at Lata's shocked face as she rose and opened the door.

Maybe Mamma would remain here too, then, like the rani and maybe she would understand that it wasn't really her fault, she thinks as she goes to find Abha.